Origami Balloon
Becoming Mei-Rose

Cheryl Moy
Illustrated by Ari Silva

The Origami Balloon

Copyright © 2022 Cheryl Moy
All Rights Reserved
First Edition
ISBN: 978-0-578-39807-5

It is forbidden to copy, reproduce, transmit or adapt this publication by any means, electronically or mechanically, unless you obtain express permission from the author. This is an independent publication. This is a work of fiction and any names or circumstances that show resemblance to reality or with actual subjects are purely coincidental. Names, places and events are the product of the author's imagination or have been used fictitiously.

Permission should be addressed in writing to Cheryl Moy at www.cheryl-moy.com.

Editor: Charlotte L. Taylor

Dedication

For all the courageous females who have a dream to write a book and share their story of what life has entailed. With laughter mixed amongst the struggle, out comes a champion.

For my loving husband, Don. For the past five years, you have encouraged me to write my story to show the real me and to wear my courage as a badge of honor. You are my lighthouse. As we continue forward, we will carry on growing in our loving life partnership as well as in business.

For my grandparents, parents, siblings and cousins. You have been an inspiration to me throughout my life, and I have so many treasured memories filled with our laughter.

For my friends, who have been with me through thick and thin. You make my life so complete, and you help me to see what I have accomplished thus far. Each one of you has been my cheerleader during this amazing journey.

For a very special lady, Pashmina P., and the delightful OAO team. I'm so glad that you are part of my life. You are a great teacher who always saw the inner light in me, and you gave me the belief that I could achieve my dream of becoming an author.

For Charlotte L. Taylor. You bring a fun, creative side to the writing world with your professionalism and wit.

For Ari. You have brought my words to life through your incredible illustrations.

Table of Contents

Mei	7
Rose	23
Thrown in at the Deep End	41
Chow Mein and a Side of Fries	57
Road Trip	69
Oh, to Be Chang'e!	83
Bunty's Cookies and Cakes	95
Life after Ai	111
A Soup for Every Occasion	131
Angel Island	143
Chinese New Year	159
A Bonding and Breaking of Hearts	177
Beetle Bugs and Bras	195
Coincidences	215
Mei-Rose	233
Please Drink Tea	245
Epilogue	267
Acknowledgements	277
About the Author	279

自爱
Mei

I woke as the early morning sun shone through the gap in my curtains, dancing its light upon my face. I could hear Ling snoring gently in her cot on the other side of the room, and as I glanced over, rubbing the sleep from my eyes, I could see her podgy little leg dangling between the bars.

I scrambled out from under my covers and popped my head through the curtains to look at the world outside. Down in the yard, Ai had just come out of his kennel, and he performed one of his great stretches that always looked so satisfying—the ones which started at the ends of his whiskers and finished at the very tips of his toes. I knocked lightly on the window, and he looked up. When he saw me gazing down at him, he wagged his bushy tail and then flopped down on the grass in the shade of the green ash tree.

My bedroom door burst open, and Wing ran in.

"It's my birthday! It's my birthday!" he sang in Cantonese, waking up Ling in the process. "Do you know how old I am now?"

I laughed and threw my pillow at him as my little sister wasted no time in clambering over the bars of her cot, wobbling as she balanced on the top of them. I rushed over to her and took her into my arms, giving her a kiss on her rosy cheek.

"You're a year behind me, dìdì!" I giggled to Wing, "So you're five!"

"Why is there such a commotion going on in here?" Māmā asked as she bustled into the room.

"Māmā," Wing sang as he danced around our mother's legs, "do you know it's my birthday?"

"Yes, my boy," Māmā said as she took Ling from me and went to open the curtains, "but there's still teeth to brush and breakfast to make. Come on … Yídòng!" And Māmā shooed my excited brother from my room. "Don't be long, Mei," she called back to me as she followed Wing out.

"I won't, Māmā," I promised as I picked up the pillow from where it had fallen and proceeded to make mine and Ling's beds. Once everything was neat and tidy, I brushed my teeth and went downstairs.

Bàba was already sitting at the kitchen table reading the daily newspaper. He patted my head as I walked past and said, "Good morning, qīn'ài de."

"Good morning, Bàba," I smiled at him, and went to collect the breakfast bowls from the cupboard to set upon the table. "I hope you had a good sleep?"

"Yes, Mei, I did. Thank you," he said, and then his head disappeared again behind his newspaper.

Māmā had already started boiling the water for our breakfast, so I fetched the dumplings from the fridge and the rice to make the congee. Then I pulled a kitchen chair next to the stove so that I could climb up and help my mother to stir the pots. I enjoyed doing this because it made me feel like a big, grown girl.

"Before you do that, Mei, could you take your sister to feed Ai please?" Māmā asked. I scrambled back down and grabbed Ling by the hand, helping her into her boots.

Outside, the day already felt humid, and I tilted my face to the sun whilst closing my eyes. I loved the warmth it gave, and I sighed deeply. A wet nose pushed into my dangling hand brought me out of my reverie, and I laughed as I looked down into Ai's expectant brown eyes.

"Okay, okay! I'll feed you, you silly dog!" I said, patting him on the head. "Oh, Ling, no!

Yuck! Spit it out!"

My little sister was sitting in the dirt with one hand in the food bag, chomping quite happily on the dried dog cereal. I ran over to her and took the bag from her, filled up Ai's bowl, and checked that he also had enough water.

"You can't be eating Ai's food, mèimei," I told a disappointed Ling as I ruffled her hair. "Our breakfast will be *much* tastier!"

Once back in the kitchen, I left Ling playing with a puzzle and came back to join Māmā at the stove. The water was boiling now, and she let me pop the pork dumplings in using a large spoon. Then she showed me how to weigh out the right amount of rice for the congee. Wing had been allowed to choose this breakfast because it was his special day; it happened to be one of my favorites too.

As breakfast was cooking, Wing laid the table mats and placed the breakfast bowls upon them before fetching the chopsticks. Whilst these eating utensils were all made of the same bamboo wood, mine had purple tips because that was my favorite color. Wing's were yellow, Ling's were green, Bàba's were red and Māmā's were blue. They brought such color to our table.

Ling finished off the task by finding the napkins to put next to our empty bowls. I loved how we all worked together to make something happen. Māmā always told me that it was the way it should be; that American children were allowed to grow lazy, and they expected their parents to fetch everything for them. "Not in our house, Mei," she would say in Cantonese. "It's not our way."

The dumplings and congee were soon ready, and they were placed in large bowls so that we could help ourselves once we were seated at the table.

"Bàba, what do you have planned today?" Māmā asked.

"Work," my father replied. "The restaurant is fully booked today. What about you, Māmā?"

"Well, I thought the children and I would take the bus to the museum today because it is Saturday. Would you like that, háizimen?"

"Yes, Māmā," Wing and I chorused. Ling was too busy attempting to put a whole pork dumpling into her mouth to pay us any attention.

"I would like to see the Ancient China exhibition please, Māmā. What about you, Wing?"

"I would like to see the dinosaurs!" Wing replied, his eyes sparkling.

"Raaaa," said Ling. "Dinosaurs!"

"Lee Ling, do not speak with your mouth full!" Bàba chided.

Once the breakfast dishes had been washed, Wing sat back down at the table once more in order to receive his birthday present. Bàba disappeared outside into the back yard before returning with a red and blue bicycle boasting a big yellow bow. I wondered how I had missed seeing that earlier. It was so shiny that even its tires seemed to sparkle!

"Happy birthday, érzi," he said. "I will teach you how to ride it tomorrow."

Wing was thrilled, and so was I. The rules of our household meant that Wing would have to share this present with me and Ling, so we would all have the chance to learn to ride a bicycle. Wing would have the first go, though, of course—it had been the same the year before when I'd been gifted my purple tricycle.

Bàba soon went off to work, and I helped Māmā to get Ling ready for our trip to the museum. My sister and I had matching summer dresses, which were red with white collars. There were also pretty white flowers dotted around on the material too. Auntie Lian had made them for us as she did every year because she was the great seamstress in our family.

Once we were all ready, my mother

checked that she had the right money for the bus and the museum, and we packed a bag with food for our lunch. I had helped Māmā prepare this the day before: shrimp spring rolls, sticky baked chicken wings, wood ear mushroom salad and steamed buns. It made my mouth water just thinking about our park picnic later.

Ling held my hand as we walked down the busy street to the bus stop. Wing was talking to Māmā about which dinosaur he really wanted to see, and his arms were waving in all directions as he spoke, but she didn't notice because she was striding ahead to ensure we didn't miss the bus.

"Lái, Ling! Come on! Stop dragging your feet, or Māmā will leave us behind," I urged my sister. "See, look how far ahead she is already!"

But Ling didn't care. She was too young to understand really, so I picked her up and sat her on my hip as best I could as I hurried after Wing and our mother.

No sooner had we caught up than the bus appeared and pulled up alongside us. Māmā asked for tickets in her broken English and then ushered us along the aisle to some empty seats at the back of the bus. I sat by the window, as I loved to watch the world speed past as we traveled. The streets were so busy with people hurrying here and there—I always played the game of wondering where they were going, and the more bizarre the ideas, the better!

We got off at our usual stop, a block from the museum. This part of town was so busy, and Māmā took Ling's hand this time whilst Wing and I did our best to navigate the sea of legs, many of which were adorned with suit trousers. It was always quite disconcerting to dodge the current of people walking in the opposite direction, especially as we couldn't actually see where we were going, and it felt like we were struggling to swim against the tide. We just kept our eyes fixed on Māmā's red coat ahead of us.

Before long, my mother and Ling veered off to the left, so I grabbed Wing's hand and did the same. We breathed a sigh of relief as we entered the cool and less-hectic foyer of the city's National History Museum. My little heart was hammering against my chest.

"Stand up tall, Mei, and straighten your dress!" Māmā said. "*Aii-ya*! Even your hair is a mess, child. Come here!"

As she proceeded to rake her expert fingers through my hair to tame it back down, I tried my best not to wriggle or wince as she pulled at the tangles. Maybe next time I should wear it up like Ling, I decided. But, I felt safer wearing it down because I could bend my head and hide behind my hair whenever I felt unsure. It was like my own personal, security curtain falling over my face and shutting out the world beyond. Therefore, having Māmā pull at it now was a small price to pay, really.

We all knew this museum so well; it was our typical haunt whenever we decided to leave the familiarity of Chinatown. Wing led the way to the dinosaur exhibition, and we all *oohed* and *aahed* at the gigantic skeletons of these prehistoric behemoths that had roamed our lands.

My favorite was the brontosaurus, as I loved the curve of its long neck as it arched over our heads. I also appreciated the fact that, despite its size, it had been considered a placid creature in its day.

Wing made a beeline for his favorite: the velociraptor. He liked that it had been fast and deadly with hollow bones and a surprising plumage of feathers; a far cry from my ancient, gentle giant.

I'm not sure if Ling had a favorite yet, although she did seem to favor the model of a trachodon—I think it reminded her of *Beautiful Day Monster* from our Sesame Street program. Māmā deemed this show educational, so we were allowed to watch it because it taught us our numbers and words and helped us to learn how to speak English.

We spent quite some time wandering around the exhibits, allowing Wing the opportunity to enlighten us with his extensive knowledge of all the different species and sub-species of these impressive beasts. I really could see him achieving his dream of becoming a paleontologist when he was older.

After a while, I tuned him out and let my mind roam to imagining myself in Pangaea, watching young dinosaurs playfully fight while their parents foraged for food. The triceratops mingled happily with the stegosauruses, and large, bat-like pterodactyls swooped overhead. I shuddered when looking at their papery-thin wings, imagining them easy to tear on rogue tree branches.

"Mei! Mei! Pay attention, child! Stop this silly daydreaming of yours," my mother complained as she slapped me on the arm, which made the prehistoric landscape disappear in an instant. "We're off to *your* room of choice now. No doubt you will show more focus there."

"Sorry, Māmā," I mumbled, and I threw Wing a smile of apology. "I was on the plain in Pangaea, playing with the baby dinosaurs," I whispered to him, and he rolled his eyes in mock despair.

"Stop whispering! It's rude," snapped my mother as she marched ahead with Ling toddling behind. "Lái! Ancient China is this way. Keep up!"

Wing grinned at me and we went hurrying after Māmā. I couldn't contain my excitement, as this was by far my favorite exhibition—museum curators had recreated parts of the Great Wall of China, and they had even built a large model of the Forbidden City.

I loved Chinese architecture. I loved Chinese history. In fact, I pretty much loved everything related to China. It made me feel proud to be part of a culture with such a rich story to share.

Whilst Māmā was busy educating Wing about the Tang dynasty, I stole the opportunity to meander around the displays by myself. I particularly enjoyed the exhibits showing the creative side of my ancestors: the paper-making and the silk painting were my favorites. I had already decided to ask my parents if they would be kind enough to gift me a silk painting set for my birthday, which was coming up in a few months time.

I loved everything about silk, and to think I could own a bit—and paint my very own piece

of it—would be a dream come true.

As I walked past the ancient emperor costumes, I longed to reach beyond the barrier cord and brush the garments with my fingertips. Embellished with gold thread and jewels, they boasted of their previous owners' wealth and social standing. They almost dripped with royalty and power, prestige and arrogance.

I found the display which heralded the history of the humble kite. First created using silk and bamboo, they also designed paper versions of many colorful shades. I was amazed to hear that kites even had a place in Medieval China's military history. I thought they were beautiful. Beautifully clever.

Glancing over at my family, I could see that Wing was still mid-lecture—and Ling was being held in a vice grip by Māmā—so I further took the opportunity to sit upon an iron bench to watch the world pass me by.

Back in Chinatown, people dressed as we did. However, in this part of the city my eyes were opened to what other people wore. Children walked past me wearing jeans and t-shirts, with trainers or funny jelly shoes on their feet. Typically these children were moaning or whining as they were pulled along by their parents, who didn't even seem to notice their ungrateful behavior.

A couple of the children who passed by looked like me, but most of the children looked nothing like me. As I sat there quietly on my bench, I tried to process how there could be so many differences in the people who lived in one city: clothes, faces, skin color. We were all so remarkably different.

A boy with blond hair glanced at me as he walked past with his mother. I gave him a tentative smile, but he just stuck his tongue out at me and stared. I bowed my head and let my curtain of security shield me from his rudeness.

"Mei? Mei! What is wrong with you today, gūniáng! You are so distracted." My mother stormed over to me, followed by a rather relieved-looking Wing, no doubt happy that his history lesson had finished.

"Sorry, Māmā," I said. "I was just watching the other children with their parents."

"Don't be getting any silly notions in that head of yours, do you hear? We have our ways and they have theirs!"

"Of course, Māmā."

"Here, take Ling. You are responsible for her until we get to the park. It is time for our lunch."

And, with that, we left the museum and its

treasures behind and ventured back out into the humid heat of the city with its unforgiving sea of human legs.

自爱
Rose

Once at the park, Māmā carefully unpacked our picnic while Wing and I smoothed out the blanket that we would be sitting upon.

Ling had discovered a Monarch butterfly and was chasing it around, trying to capture it and bring it home as a pet. It was fun to watch her clap her hands each time as she missed, and the unperturbed butterfly continued its search for the sweetest nectar in the park's flora.

"Ling, come! Lunch is ready!" Māmā said as she patted the blanket beside her.

Ling ran over and sat down, reaching out a chubby hand for the nearest spring roll on the tinfoil next to her.

"*Ai-ya*! What must you say first, child? Where are your manners?" said Māmā.

"Thank you for food, Māmā," said Ling. "It yummy!" and she beamed up at our mother.

The food was indeed delicious. Whilst trying not to get too sticky with the chicken wings, I watched as other children walked down the path next to us, devouring hotdogs and burgers. Although I had never tasted either of these American foods, I had to admit that our picnic seemed more appealing with its vibrancy of color and plethora of appetizing scents.

Once our stomachs were full, I helped my mother to wrap up the leftovers.

"Māmā, please may I feed the ducks some of the steamed buns?"

"One or two. No more. The rest we can have with our dinner tonight. And take Ling. Be sure to keep her away from the side of the water though."

So Ling and I left our brother, who was lying on his back trying to spot animal shapes in the clouds above, and we skipped over to the park's big pond. The luscious reeds, which grew around most of its perimeter, were taller than us both, and I loved how this made me feel as though I was exploring in the Amazon rainforest.

We found a natural gap in the foliage and carefully made our way to the water's edge.

"That's close enough," I said to Ling. "Māmā would be so cross with me if you fell in!"

I handed my sister one of the steamed buns, and I started to break up the other one, flinging the tiny morsels into the water as far as I could, hoping to encourage some of the ducks over. I turned around to make sure that Ling was doing the same, only to see her chewing.

"Ling! The bun is for the ducks!"

"But I like bun. Bun yummy! Ducks don't want bun," Ling said with a frown upon her little face.

I gave her my crossest look and put my hand on my hip like I had seen Māmā do a thousand times.

"Lee Ling! You will feed the bun to the ducks now, or I will take you back and you can stay with Wing!"

Ling began to cry, but she did as I said. She was very ungracious with her offering though—I thought she was maybe trying to throw the bread *at* the few ducks that had come over to us, rather than *for* them.

"Well done, xiǎo mèimei, you did a great job," I said as I smiled at her, but Ling continued to look sulky all the way back to Māmā.

爱

That evening, before dinner, I set up the table for Mahjong. This was a family favorite because it was our special time—the time when we would all be together, no matter what, sharing our news of the day.

I ran my thumb over the white acrylic tiles as I took them from their bag. They were so tactile, and I loved the colorful Chinese characters and symbols—the Winds set was my favorite, with the Seasons a close second.

I turned each tile face down, shuffled them well and then dealt 13 of them to each corner of the table, ready for play to begin. As I dealt the pieces out, there was a satisfying clinking sound when acrylic met wood.

Ling was still too young for this game, but Wing and I were learning the rules every evening, courtesy of Bàba. Wing seemed to be a natural, and he was quick to pick up the tricks and skills to win; my efforts were always bumbling ones, so I relied more upon luck than anything else. But, I loved the connection that this game gave me to my family. The chatter always flowed, and by the time the game had finished, we all knew what had been the highs and lows of everyone's day.

Once the Mahjong table was prepared, I went outside to see Ai.

We hadn't ever planned on getting a dog, but Ai had found us and claimed us (he had arrived in our back yard one day and had then refused to leave). Bàba had tried everything to discourage him—from shouting at Ai to throwing things at him—but the dog just kept coming back. And his perseverance had paid off, for we could all see what a lovely nature he had despite the fact he was a scruffy stray.

So Bàba had relented, with the firm understanding that the dog would live in the back yard—he was never to come into the house. Wing and I had been thrilled, and we had helped Bàba to build a beautiful kennel, which we made snug in the winter with lots of blankets. We also fixed plastic strips to the doorway so that they would shelter Ai from any wind or rain when he was sleeping, but which would allow him to come and go as he pleased.

Ai seemed very happy with the arrangement, and from that day on, he became a much-loved member of our family. His coat grew glossy and thick, and soon he had put on the perfect amount of weight.

He had also become my best friend, and I spent many hours cuddled up to him in his kennel once all my chores had been done, and I would share with him my inner-most thoughts and feelings. Today was no exception.

"It's funny," I said as he placed his head in my lap and gazed up at me with those brown, soulful eyes, "how that boy thought it was

okay to stick his tongue out at me."

Ai gave my hand a sympathetic lick, and then replaced his head on my knee so that I could resume twiddling his ear.

"All I did was smile at him. Shouldn't I have done that? Was I being too friendly, maybe? But smiles are nice."

I sighed. I didn't have a lot of experience playing with other children, and the only children I *was* familiar with were my siblings or my cousins. Sesame Street made everything look so easy—the children on there were always laughing and smiling, so I really couldn't understand the boy's reaction. And it surprised me now to realize how hurt I felt by his behavior.

"Mei," my mother's voice came from the back door. "Bàba is home and ready for the game of Mahjong."

I wrapped my arms around Ai's neck and buried my face in his shaggy fur as I gave him one last squeeze.

"Night, night, Ai. I love you."

The dog nibbled my hand and then stood up and stretched. As I left the kennel, he circled three times on the spot where I had been sitting, and then he flopped down upon it, tucked his nose under his tail and closed his eyes.

"Why must you sit in the kennel with the

dog? You'll end up with fleas!" my mother chided as I met her at the back door.

"Ai gives the best cuddles, Māmā."

My mother tutted and shook her head at me as she gave my clothes a quick brush down with her hand, no doubt to remove any lingering dog hairs. She then ushered me inside to my waiting family, who were sitting at the Mahjong table with their tiles and their steaming cups of tea.

爱

The next morning, there was great excitement as it was the day that Wing would learn to ride the new bicycle. Bàba didn't work on Sundays, so later we would do what we always did and visit Nǎinai and Yéyé, who were our paternal grandparents. Therefore, we were all up at the crack of dawn to get as much practice time in with the bicycle before we headed over to their house.

Bàba had already adjusted the saddle for Wing, and he was quick to encourage my brother to begin. It was nice to have these moments with Bàba because he didn't usually spend a lot of time playing with us in the yard. We knew he loved us, but he preferred to sit on the sidelines, quietly watching our development; always ready to reprimand us if we stepped out of line.

As Wing began to peddle, my father walked beside him, holding on to the back of the saddle.

"Faster, érzi!" Bàba said. "Peddle faster or you will fall when I let go."

Wing's legs went round and round as he tried to do as our father demanded, and his cheeks began to pink up. He had to maneuver corners too so that he didn't run out of space. On the third straight run, Bàba let go, much to Wing's horror. My hand flew to my mouth as I watched my little brother wobble, which made the handlebars shake, and then he toppled over and landed with a crash.

"Up! Up! Again," my father said, but Wing was crying in the dirt.

"Stop that silliness, and get back onto your bicycle," Bàba said as my brother sniffled and wiped his eyes with the back of his hand.

I could see some blood coloring the fabric of Wing's trousers, but he didn't dare let Bàba see that he wanted to give up and fix his knee. So up he got, dusted himself down, picked up his bike and tried again.

Seven more times he fell, and seven more

The Origami Balloon

times I saw his bottom lip tremble. But I was so proud of my brother because, on the eighth time of getting back onto his bicycle, he mastered the skill and beamed as he cycled a wobbly circuit around our back yard. Ling and I clapped, and Bàba gave Wing a proud slap on the back. He'd done it!

"Lái! It's time to go!" Māmā said as she appeared at the back door. "Aiiiiiii-ya, érzi! Your clothes!"

Sunday lunch was always my favorite meal of the week because, not only was it a Chinese banquet fit for royalty, it was the day we got to spend time with my uncles, aunts and cousins. My favorite cousin was Ju, who was three years older than me. I followed her everywhere like a puppy, and to be fair, she didn't seem to mind.

Under Māmā's watchful eye, we all rushed to dress in our Sunday best. Ling and I wore our navy-blue pinafore dresses with crisp, starched white blouses beneath them. On our feet, we wore white socks and our closed-toe sandals. Wing wore a blue-and-white checked shirt and his smart navy-blue cords.

Māmā approached me with a brush and proceeded to pull it none-too-gently through my hair.

"I think you should have your hair in pigtails today, Mei," she said. "I'm fed up of all these tangles."

"Oh please, Māmā. Please let me wear it down."

But Māmā had made up her mind, and my hair was dutifully scraped into bunches, just like Ling's. And so we were all ready to begin our walk through the streets to where Năinai and Yéyé lived.

The cornflower-blue skies were cloudless, and it seemed that everyone from our district was enjoying a walk in the sunshine. Neighbors waved to us and wished us a good day, and we returned the happy sentiment. I noticed other children of a similar age to us in their Sunday best, walking down the street with their parents and heading out to visit *their* relatives no doubt; it was a family day for all the residents of Chinatown.

As we turned into my grandparents' street, we saw Ju and my uncle and aunt getting out of their car.

"May I go to Ju, please, Māmā?" I asked, and my mother nodded to me as she waved to her sister-in-law, Auntie Lian.

I skipped up to my cousin and gave her a hug.

"Wing got a bicycle for his birthday, and Bàba taught him how to ride it this morning! I watched, so I think I know how to do it too. Wing will help me next time," I said in Cantonese.

"Oh, clever Wing!" my cousin beamed as we followed our parents into the house.

After we had shared greetings with my other uncles and aunts too, all of my cousins and I were given the chance to play hide-and-seek in the yard. Năinai and Yéyé had an enormous area behind their house where many mature trees and shrubs grew. This meant that there were many fantastic hiding places if you knew where to look. Yéyé also had two large sheds for his hobbies of pottery and painting, but we weren't allowed in there in case we damaged anything. Still, the buildings offered further places for a small child to conceal themselves from the searcher.

Ju was the searcher first, and as we listened to her count in Cantonese to 50, the rest of us squealed with joy and ran off in different directions, all eager to be the last to be found. I burrowed underneath a blue hydrangea bush, hoping that my dress would help me to blend in. Just as I settled myself, careful not to crease my pinafore, I heard Ju yell that she was coming to find us. I stifled a giggle as a knot of excitement formed in my chest.

As it transpired, I wasn't found last, but second-to-last, so I made a note to remember that hidey-hole for next time we played. It was such fun being with my cousins. We were about to decide on a game of tag, when Năinai opened the back door and called for us to come in for lunch. The feast was about to begin.

My mouth began watering as soon as I entered the dining room—the old, rosewood table was almost groaning under the weight of the delicacies presented upon it. There was fried rice, Peking duck, chow mein with rice noodles, and scallion pancakes. I could see Kung Pao chicken and stinky tofu. There were large baozi with soy sauce dip and char siu, and sitting in the center of the table was a huge pot of wonton soup. My eyes devoured it all, and my stomach rumbled in anticipation.

As we sat down to eat, we said our thanks for our food and passed around our bowls to be filled. The smell of the cooking was intoxicating—Năinai was the best cook I knew, although I'd never say as much to my mother. My grandmother had told me that her own mother had taught her how to make all of these dishes when she grew up in the province of Guangdong, which was on the coast of southeast China.

I loved listening to stories of Nǎinai's childhood, although sometimes she would become so immersed in her storytelling that she would forget I was there; she would get a faraway look in her eye as if she were speaking to the ghosts of her past instead.

There was always a great buzz around the table during these weekly family feasts. There was so much love and respect brought to the gathering and, as I looked at each of the faces there, I realized that this was my world; my everything.

And then everything changed.

"Mei," Bàba began. "We have some important, exciting news that we wanted to share with you today."

I stopped eating and realized that everyone was looking at me. All of the adults had the same expression, which let me know that they were all in on the secret. I looked at Ju, and she smiled at me too, whilst Wing just shrugged when I glanced at him. Clearly he was as much in the dark as I was.

"Yes, Bàba?"

"Māmā and I have decided that it is time for you to start school."

But I do schooling at home with Māmā, Wing and Ling, Bàba."

I couldn't comprehend what *starting school* meant, for every day Māmā religiously taught us our Chinese characters and numbers, and we watched Sesame Street to learn how to speak to our American neighbors. Even our Mahjong games taught us math.

"No, nǚ'ér," Bàba said, "American school. You are starting tomorrow at Oakenfield Academy."

Oakenfield Academy was a school that we passed on our bus trips to the museum, so I was able to picture it in my mind. It was just outside Chinatown, and it seemed to have cheerful artwork posted in windows, so that made me happy, but still ...

"Well, say something, child!" said Năinai. "Aren't you excited?"

"I'm not sure, Năinai. I don't know anyone there, and I'm ... I'm used to being with Wing and Ling. Are ... Are they coming too?"

"Don't be silly, Mei," said Māmā. "They will continue with homeschooling. Wing will start American school next year. You will make friends, so there is no need to make a fuss about it."

"Of course, Māmā," I said, and I bowed my head, forgetting that my security curtain had been imprisoned within hair bands.

"Don't worry, Mei. School is fun! I love going to mine," said Ju as she squeezed my hand under the table.

"Can I not go to yours? Then I'll have you there and it … it won't seem so scary."

"Tíng xiàlái! Enough!" said Bàba, and I knew the conversation was over. "You will be starting tomorrow at Oakenfield Academy, and you will go by the name of Rose."

My father then returned to his conversation with my Uncle Bao, offering me no further clarification as to why I would be called by a new name.

My young brain exploded with a thousand questions. Only minutes ago, I had been looking around the table feeling safe and content in my world; the world which had made sense to me. Now, I was spiraling into a panic. Had I done something wrong that they were sending me away? Why was my name not okay for school? I had only ever been *Mei*, so how could I be *Rose* too? My eyes began to burn and prickle. Ju took pity on me once more.

"This is typical, don't worry" she said as everyone else continued with their own conversations, oblivious to my world imploding around me. "Only my family calls me by my Chinese name. Everyone else calls me Sarah."

"But why? Ju is a beautiful name! And I like being Mei!"

"You will always be Mei. You'll just be Rose too. At least they chose a pretty name."

"But I don't understand ... why do I *have* to be Rose?"

"My father told me it was because western people find it hard to say our Chinese names, although yours and mine are quite easy to say. But, because of this, a tradition started to help get rid of the difficulty people had, and so we are given western names when we start American school."

"Why can't they just translate our Chinese names into a western name so that we can stay the same person?"

"You *will* stay the same person, silly! Sometimes the translation can go wrong, and a beautiful Chinese name can have an ugly western word. Or, sometimes there is no straight translation. This was the easiest way to fix the problem, trust me."

I wasn't sure that I agreed with her, but there was nothing more to say. The die had been cast, and when I woke up the next day, I would be known as Rose, and my life would be irrevocably changed.

自爱
Thrown in at the Deep End

As the dawn shone orangey-purple hues through the weave of the blanket I had hidden under, I considered the thoughts that had been rattling around in my head since I had woken up, several hours earlier. What if I missed my family? What if no one wanted to be my friend? What if my teacher was scary? These musings would not settle, and my stomach was in knots.

I heard my bedroom door creak open.

"Up, Mei. We have lots to do before we get you to school. Wake Ling up, and make sure that you both brush your teeth before you come downstairs." There was a pause. "Do you hear me, gūniáng?"

I heard the curtains rattle on their pole as my mother pulled them fully open, and then the blanket was snatched from over my face.

"I said up. Now!"

"Yes, Māmā," I said, reluctant to admit the day had begun. However, there was no use in trying to deny the inevitable.

I threw my legs out of bed and used my feet to search for my slippers. I could hear Ling yawning as she began to awake, and then she squeaked as she stretched her arms high above her head. She was so sweet when she first woke up in the morning, and I smiled at her as her little face popped up over the bars of her cot.

"Morning, mèimei," I said as I helped her out. "Let's make our beds and then go and brush our teeth, shall we?"

"Breakfast," Ling said.

"Yes, breakfast afterwards."

"Breakfast now. Ling hungry."

"You're always hungry," I laughed as I straightened the blankets on our beds. "Come on."

Downstairs, Māmā was putting granola into bowls for us. Maybe the fact that our whole daily routine was changing meant that she didn't want to have to worry about cooking a breakfast for us that morning.

Wing was already laying the table, and Bàba was sitting at the head of it, reading his daily newspaper. I went to the drawer to get some spoons.

"Morning, Mei," Bàba said. "Did you sleep well? Are you ready for your new adventure?"

"I ... *ermm* ... yes, thank you Bàba."

There was no point in saying that I hadn't, as it was already clear that my family thought that I was making a huge fuss about nothing; I would only make them cross by saying that I was feeling worried. So, I smiled at my father and went outside to feed Ai.

My faithful companion was already lying stretched out in the shade under the ash tree, so I sat down on the grass next to him. His tail started wagging as I spoke.

"Oh, Ai," I said. "I'm so worried. What if no one likes me at my new school? What if I get lost when I go to the bathroom? Māmā and Bàba say that I'm being silly and that I'll love it, but I'm not so sure. What if I hate it?"

Ai sat up, cocked his head and looked at me square in the eye for several moments as if considering his most helpful reply. He then leant forward and gave me a slobbery lick all the way from my chin up to my forehead. I couldn't help but laugh.

"You're so right!" I said as I wiped his drool from my face with my sleeve. "There's no point worrying about it until I get there. Maybe I *will* make some friends and it'll be as Ju says it is.

Maybe it *will* be fun. Thanks, Ai! You're the best!"

After filling up his food and water bowls and giving his head one last scratch, I ran back into the house to get washed up before breakfast. My family was already sitting at the table waiting to start.

"Lái! Lee Mei! Don't make us wait for you. Hurry!" Bàba said.

爱

Once the breakfast dishes had been washed, I ran back upstairs to get ready for school. Māmā had laid my clothes on my bed ready, and I trailed my fingertips over the top of them. I was to wear another smart pinafore, dark green this time, with a white blouse underneath. Māmā had chosen my white socks with the green bows on to compliment the pinafore, and I had already seen my black Mary Jane shoes polished to within an inch of their lives and waiting for me by the front door.

Just as I was doing up the last strap on my dress, Wing came in and sat on my bed. He looked a little lost.

"It's going to be strange today," he mumbled.

"It'll be okay," I smiled at him. "At least you'll be coming home again and you're not getting left somewhere you don't know."

"Are you scared?"

I looked at my little brother and caught my bottom lip between my teeth. I could feel the tears threatening to break free, but I remembered what I had said to Ai.

"I *am* worried," I admitted, "but I also think that it could be fun? Ju likes her school, and I like to learn things, so maybe it'll be okay. I hope so, anyway."

"Well, I think you are brave, jiějiě. I wish I could go with you."

"Yes, me too. Then I wouldn't be worried at all!"

Our mother called for us to hurry. We were getting the bus to school, and it was clear that she was anxious about missing it, so I helped Ling into her dress.

"*Aiii-ya*! Your hair!" Māmā said to me once we came downstairs. "Oh, there is no time to put it up, but stand still while I brush it!"

As the bus pulled up outside Oakenfield

Academy, I had my nose pressed against the window. I could see so many children milling around; children of many different nationalities. They were running and laughing, and they disappeared into the school's front doors with barely a goodbye glance at their parents. My heart was in my throat as Māmā motioned for me and my siblings to follow her off the bus.

We maneuvered our way through the crowds and up the steps of the school. Although the doors were painted a cheerful yellow, the space between them looked like a large, dark mouth just waiting to devour me whole. I felt hands slip into both of mine, and I glanced left to right at Wing and Ling, giving their hands a grateful squeeze in return. Even my normally oblivious little sister seemed somber; she sensed the gravity of the situation too.

Māmā strode ahead and ushered us into the school office, which was situated just inside the entrance. I was too busy craning my neck to see up the corridor to hear what was being said, but before I knew it, my mother was telling me that she would be back to pick me up at 3 p.m. She gave me a brisk nod and then left, with Wing and Ling glancing over their shoulders at me as they followed her out. I gave them a cheery little wave, trying to swallow the tears that were once again promising to spill.

"Hello, Rose. It's nice to meet you," said the lady who was standing in front of me. I hadn't even noticed her, and I jumped. "My name is Mrs. Bundy, and I'm the school secretary. I'll take you to your class now. Your teacher is called Mrs. Applegate."

Mrs. Bundy then set off down the corridor, leading me past many closed, colorful doors, behind which I could hear laughter and the chanting of numbers in English. It reminded me of Sesame Street.

Finally we came to an orange door with painted, cardboard stars upon it. A different child's face was stuck upon each star, smiling back at me. So many faces! And then I noticed that one star was faceless, and I wondered if it was for me.

Mrs. Bundy knocked on the door twice and opened it without waiting for a reply. Peeking across the threshold from behind her, I saw a huge room with a blue carpet and lots of tables with activities set out on them. There seemed to be all sorts of crafts, building blocks, lined paper and pencils, counters and plastic numbers. These were the only items that I recognized; other objects lay upon other tables, but I didn't have a clue what they were for.

Children's pictures of rainbow dragons and glittered flowers adorned the walls, and from the ceiling hung homemade paper tissue crafts, which were twirling and fluttering in the breeze from the open windows.

Down at the front of the classroom, the teacher sat on a comfy chair with a big blue book in one hand and a pen in the other, and many children were sitting cross-legged in semi-circular rows on the floor at her feet.

"Mrs. Applegate, here is your new student," said Mrs. Bundy as she gestured for me to sit down at the edge of the last semi-circle next to a freckle-faced boy with ginger hair. He shuffled over to give me more room.

"Ah yes, thank you, Mrs. Bundy. We were just taking attendance."

My new teacher smiled at me. It seemed a genuine smile, and I liked how she wore her hair in two braids, one either side of her face. I gave her a shy smile in return.

"Benjamin Goode."

"Here, miss."

"Melissa Jackson."

"Here, miss."

"Rose Lee."

There was a protracted silence, and soon I began to wonder whether Rose Lee was poorly today. I started fiddling with the ribbons on my socks while I waited for the next name to be called. I was curious about the learning I was going to be doing, and I wanted to get on with it.

"Rose Lee."

While I waited, I glanced over at the rest of the children, who all seemed to be staring back at me. It was too much attention, and I bowed my head to let my curtain of hair cover my face. The freckle-faced boy gave me a nudge in the ribs; it was quite sore, and all of a sudden, it all felt far too strange.

"*Rose Lee*," my teacher said again, and I looked up at her in bewilderment, trying to fathom out why she wouldn't just go on to the next name.

I could feel my heart starting to beat faster, and I felt a little dizzy. I couldn't understand why this Rose Lee wasn't answering—she must be there if the teacher kept saying her name. It was so confusing and the room was starting to feel a little too warm. I wished this Rose girl, wherever she was, would just answer so that we could get on with the day.

Mrs. Applegate gave me an expectant look as I continued to search her face for answers, and in that moment, the penny dropped. *I* was Rose Lee. Lee Mei was now Rose Lee, and *that's* why

The Origami Balloon

they were all staring. Rose Lee wasn't poorly; she was just struggling to adjust to her new identity.

I felt so foolish, but I worked hard to swallow my embarrassment.

"Here, miss."

Mrs. Applegate frowned a little at me, but her focus soon shifted to a brown-haired girl with glasses sitting at the front, so I bent my head to shield my peers from the tear that had escaped and was marking a lonely trail down my face.

"Kelly Norman."

"Here miss."

爱

After attendance had finished, the children were assigned their tasks, and Mrs. Applegate called me over to her. She slowly explained the daily routine of the class, and she called over a little girl who had beautiful cornrows in her hair.

"This is Bethany, and she is going to be your buddy until you get used to things around here. Bethany, please show Rose where she can hang up her coat and school bag and where the restroom is. See if you can help her to find her locker too."

Mrs. Applegate then went off to sort out a

squabble by the toy cars, and Bethany took me by the hand and led me to where lots of other coats were hanging. She showed me my hook, and I hung up my coat and bag before we went off to see the cloakroom.

Bethany was lovely. Once we had found my locker, she led me back to where she had been working at the craft table creating symmetrical butterflies. She showed me how to paint one side of the paper and then fold the sheet in half to print the other side.

Another girl drifted over, and Bethany introduced me to her friend, Faye. The two of them started asking me lots of questions about who I was, where I came from and what I liked to do. The problem was that I didn't know a lot of English because we only spoke Cantonese at home; I had learned the extent of my English from watching the television.

The girls tried their best, but after a while they began talking to each other instead. They weren't being mean; they just didn't know how to get the answers from me that they wanted to find out. They kept looking over at me as I created my own butterflies, smiling when they caught my eye, but after a while they wandered off and left me by myself.

At lunchtime, Bethany came to find me

again and told me where to line up for school lunches. I showed her my packed lunch, and I noted her surprise. I seemed to be the only child in my class who had one. She pointed to a table where I could sit and wait for her and Faye.

As the tables filled up around me, I opened up my wrapped food. Tears prickled my eyes for the umpteenth time as I recognized the leftovers from yesterday's meal at Năinai's and Yéyé's. It already felt like a lifetime ago that I had been playing in their yard, and despite being surrounded by hundreds of children, I had never felt more alone.

Bethany and Faye came and sat with me just as I was taking a bite of a scallion pancake, and I could see them staring at my chow mein and rice noodles. Faye said something, and Bethany giggled. Then they started eating their hotdogs and fries, followed by a small bowl of pink ice-cream.

All the while they chattered, but they spoke so quickly that I didn't stand a chance of understanding what they were saying. Only a few words I recognized, and it was now that I realized Sesame Street hadn't prepared me for American school as much as Māmā had hoped.

The afternoon passed. I entertained myself by playing with the dominoes and the counters because, by that time, most of the children in class had given up trying to communicate with me. I was very much a square peg trying to fit into a round hole, and *everything* about me was so different from every other child there; from the food I had eaten to the clothes I was wearing. On top of all of that, my lack of conversational English now meant that I was an anomaly they couldn't even *begin* to understand.

At home time, I had to resist the urge to run to my mother—she would have disapproved of that lack of decorum. Mrs. Applegate explained as best she could how my very limited English had alienated me on my first day, and she gave Māmā a pack of English words linked to pictures that I had to learn.

"Once she starts improving her English, I'm sure she'll make lots of friends," my teacher said. "The rest of the children are a lovely bunch, so give them all time and she'll soon settle in very well."

All the way home, I didn't utter a word as I stared at the gray world outside. While Ling sat on my knee and hummed away to herself, Wing kept looking at me as if he wanted to say something, but each time, he changed his mind.

Once through the front door, Māmā told me to get changed and to hang my clothes up ready for the next day. Then I was to complete my normal chores and begin to learn the words I had been given. My mother sat with me as we made awkward efforts to pronounce them properly, and after a while, I was finally allowed some free time before Bàba came home.

There was only one place where I wanted to be; only one place where I felt I could open up and let my true feelings out.

As I sat in Ai's kennel with his comforting head on my shoulder, I clung on to my dog and buried my face in his scruffy fur. I sobbed and sobbed as though my heart was breaking. And maybe it was.

自爱
Chow Mein and a Side of Fries

Over the next few years, school did improve. With Māmā pushing me to learn my vocabulary every day, I was soon able to keep up with the conversations between my peers.

By the time I had reached 3rd grade, I had a small friendship group that I belonged to, which included Bethany, Faye and a Portuguese girl named Filipa.

"Remember the day you started?" said Bethany one lunchtime. "You were so quiet. I mean, you're *still* quiet now, but back then you wouldn't even say a word!"

Faye giggled at the memory whilst Filipa grabbed my hand and gave it a squeeze. She understood. She had started at Oakenfield Academy a year after me when her family had relocated from Lisbon to America. She too had been given the vocabulary cards to learn, and I had made a promise to myself that I wouldn't let her feel like I did during those first few months. So, from her very first day, I encouraged her to join our group, and I was by her side in everything.

"I know," I said to Bethany, "but remember I speak Cantonese at home, so it was all a bit scary to begin with."

"Oh, it must have been!" said Bethany. "But you speak English really well now!"

My head dropped as my cheeks flushed. Bethany's comment had been said in kindness, but all it had done was remind me of those dark weeks of uncertainty and sadness that I had endured. I never wanted to feel that way again. At home, I had even helped to prepare Wing by making him read the vocabulary cards with me, so that when he had started school the year after me, he was confident in his English and had been able to make lots of friends from the start.

A hand reached over my shoulder, interrupting my reminiscences. It roughly grabbed my lunchbox so that one of my spring rolls fell onto the floor.

"What weird stuff have you got today then?" Joshua Parker said, poking his finger into my noodles and moving them around.

"*Eww* ... looks like worms, and it stinks!"

He dropped my box back onto the table in front of me and went off, laughing with his friends. I could feel the raspberry blush creep up my neck and onto my face.

"Don't listen to him," Filipa said as she picked up the spring roll from the floor and placed it on the table next to her plate. "He's an idiot."

"I thought you were going to speak to your mom about letting you have school lunches," said Faye. "That way he can't tease you anymore."

"I know," I said, "but Māmā takes pride in cooking our lunches. It's her way of showing us how much she loves us. It's very much part of who she is. Who *we* are as a family. I don't want to upset her."

"Oh, Rose," said Bethany. "Does she even know you're being made fun of because of your food?"

I stared down at the remains of my meal — the food that I couldn't now finish — and shook my head. There was no way of explaining it to my friends so that they would understand. Food was so important to the Chinese culture; it was integral to our identity. Yet Bethany was right; it was making me an easy target for the school bullies, and Māmā would be appalled by that.

"I'll speak to her about it tonight," I said as the school bell rang for our next classes.

爱

That evening, I gazed at the bubbling pot containing the rice for dinner as I tried to pluck up the courage to speak to Māmā about my lunches. It felt so unfair because I actually loved the food that she packed for me, but the bullying was becoming unbearable. Nearly every day, I felt like I had to try and gobble down my food before the 4th graders, and Joshua, came into the lunch hall.

Wing was chopping vegetables at the table, and Ling was setting out our dinner bowls. Māmā had gone upstairs to put away some washing, and I took some deep breaths to steady my nerves.

"Stir it, Mei! Don't just look at it, nǚ'ér. The rice will stick to the bottom!" Māmā said as she came back into the kitchen.

"Yes, Māmā," I said. "Māmā?"

"What is it? You've been acting funny ever since you came home. Are you feeling unwell?"

"No, not really. I just need to talk to you about something and I don't want to make you sad," I said.

"Well, what is it? I hope you have been behaving at school."

"Of course, Māmā. It's nothing like that. It's about my lunches. Would you be *very* cross if I asked to have school lunches?"

The silence was deafening as my mother stared at me; it was as if I had just told her I'd committed a murder. Wing stopped chopping.

"Oh *here* we go!" she eventually said, eyes blazing. "I wondered how long it would be before you wanted American food and no doubt American clothes. You are *not* American, Mei. You are *Chinese*!"

"Well, I *am* a bit American, Māmā. Wing, Ling and I were born here, and Wing and I go to an American school."

"Nǐ zěnme gǎn! Don't you dare disrespect me like that!"

"I'm sorry, Māmā. I didn't mean to be rude, but there is a bully at school who keeps teasing me about my lunches. It doesn't matter how much I love them, which I do! He keeps being nasty to me because my lunches are different to everyone else's!"

My mother took a long, hard look at me, her lips a thin line and her hand on her hip. When she exhaled, she visibly softened and sat down at the table. She pointed to the chair opposite for me to sit down too.

"How long has this been going on for?"

"Since kindergarten," I mumbled.

"Oh, Mei! Why did you not tell me before?"

"Because I didn't want to upset you, but my friends think you should know. And I think they are right. Would you mind if I had school lunches, Māmā? I promise you they won't be as tasty as yours, but at least the bullies will leave me alone then."

My mother looked over at Wing, who was still standing motionless with the chopping knife in his hand.

"And what about you, érzi? Do you feel the same way?"

"I do, Māmā. They try to tease me sometimes too, but I have more friends to help me than Mei does. I think it would be better for Ling too, when she starts kindergarten next week. It'll help us all to fit in a bit better, I think."

"But why should you want to fit in? You should be proud to be Chinese!" Māmā said, her voice rising.

"We *are* proud," said Wing calmly. "But we also want to have a quiet life at school."

My mother glanced between the two of us several times and then nodded once.

"I will discuss it with Bàba tonight, and we will decide. For now, I want to hear no more talk about it."

"Yes, Māmā."

The next day I was giddy with excitement as I stood in the lunch queue at school. I still couldn't quite believe that Māmā and Bàba had taken on board what Wing and I had said, but I was so grateful that they had listened. I was going to be able to have a lunch that was unremarkable enough not to have someone stick their grubby finger in it, and I couldn't wait. Also, Faye had told me that Mac n' Cheese was on the menu — this was one American dish that I *had* wanted to try.

A week later, a pale-faced Ling was beginning kindergarten. I had schooled her on her vocabulary, like I had with Wing, and so I knew that she would be okay. She was such an outgoing, bubbly girl — a completely different personality to my own — so I knew that she would excel. But, I understood her first day nerves.

Māmā and Bàba had continued with the flower theme and given her *Lily* as her western name. She had seemed to accept this much more readily than I had three years earlier, but then she had seen both Wing and I go through it, so she had been expecting it. It also helped that Bethany's little sister, Briana, was going to be in the same class, so Ling would have a friend straight away.

Māmā didn't come in with us, so it was up to me to take Ling to her new class. She skipped in quite happily and gave Mrs. Applegate the biggest smile. As the door closed, concealing her from sight, I heard my little sister's voice ring out, clear as a bell.

"Hello, my name's Lily. Who are you?"

That summer when the semester was over, it was time for our family vacation; our great road trip which we took every year. Năinai and Yéyé, Auntie Lian, Uncle Bao and Ju, and Bàba, Māmā, Wing, Ling and I all travelled together in two cars, driving to our chosen city as we explored America and Canada.

This year we were going to visit Washington D.C. and I couldn't wait. As much as I loved learning all about my Chinese heritage, I also was fascinated by the other part of who I was; Rose, the American.

There was always great excitement surrounding these trips, as we would book into motels and hotels throughout the vacation, which was always a thrilling adventure.

This year was going to be even better—I was told that Bàba would share with Wing, Māmā would share with Ling, and Ju and I were to be given a room of our own to share as long as it was situated in between the adults' rooms. Ju and I felt very grown up, and we looked forward to being able gossip into the early hours of the morning.

The day before we were due to leave, I went to spend some time with Ai in his kennel. I was going to miss him so much, but I reassured myself that it was only going to be for two weeks. A neighbor had agreed to feed Ai for us, so we knew he would be well looked after in our absence. But, still ...

"Shall I bring you back a nice new collar?" I asked as I scratched him behind his ear. "Will you be *very* lonely without me?"

Ai rolled onto his back, inviting me to tickle his tummy. I hoped that he wasn't going to punish me for going away like he had last year. On my return then, he had made it very clear that he wasn't impressed—every time I had gone to spend time with him, he had walked a little way away from me and then resolutely sat with his back to me. If I went over to where he had moved to, he would get up and move to another part of the back yard. He had been in such a huff, and the message had been loud and clear: You should not have left me.

This punishment had gone on for a full week before he had finally forgiven me; half the length of time I had been away. This was why I was trying to sweeten him up now.

"Or maybe you would like a thick doggy coat for winter? A plaid one?"

Ai got to his feet, yawned and then licked my cheek. It would seem that a plaid coat for winter was exactly what he needed.

"Mei, are you out there?" Māmā's voice came from the back door. "You need to come and finish packing your things, gūniáng."

"Maybe I can squeeze you into my suitcase, Ai. What do you think?" I laughed, and Ai gave a little bark. "I'll come and feed you tomorrow morning before we go, boy. Love you!"

And with that, I gave him one last cuddle and ran into the house to finish all of the chores I had to do in order to prepare for our vacation.

自爱
Road Trip

The next morning, the sun was just creeping above the rooftops as I snuggled up to Ai in his kennel. My family and I were going to set off on our road trip straight after breakfast because we had a six-hour journey ahead of us before we arrived at our stop-over motel. We would be arriving in Washington D.C. the next day in the late afternoon.

"I promise to miss you every single day," I said as I buried my face in the scruffy fur on his neck, "and I'm going to bring you home the nicest, red plaid coat that I can find. It'll be all woolly on the inside too so that you are really cozy this winter."

I hoped that my loyal friend understood. I had even asked Bàba if we could bring Ai with us, but the reply to that was not something I would wish to share with my dog; it would only offend him. So, I was left having to fit in two weeks' worth of scratches and cuddles before we left.

"Mei, are you out here?" said Ling. "Māmā asked me to find you so that you can help to cook the youtiao for breakfast."

I poked my head out of the kennel doorway and grinned at my sister.

"I'll be right in, mèimei. I'm just saying goodbye to Ai."

"You and that dog," Ling laughed as she skipped back up the steps and disappeared into the house.

"So, my boy, the time has come! Please don't be mad at me. I'll be back before you know it, and I'll come to find you straight away because I'll have missed you so much. Look after yourself, and please don't bite Mrs. Huang. We were lucky that she agreed to look after you again after last time! You know how Bàba will get if you cause trouble."

And with a last scratch behind his ear, I dropped a kiss upon his nose and crawled out of the kennel.

爱

An hour later, the last bag was being strapped to the roof of the car. Năinai, Yéyé, Uncle Bao,

Auntie Lian and Ju were traveling in one car, and my family and I were traveling in the other. The motel we had pre-booked was just outside Cleveland, and Ju and I were excited for our sleepover.

On the journey, Wing, Ling and I played Chinese Checkers or devised our own games, such as making up stories about where all the cars on the highway were going. We also liked playing the game where everyone picked a car color and the person who saw the most cars of their color would win. Red cars seemed to be the winner most times.

Hours later—just as Ling was beginning to get irritable, moaning about her lack of space and the fact her legs were fidgety—Bàba announced that we had arrived.

We pulled up next to Uncle Bao's car in front of a gray building, which had three floors of identical front-facing doors that were accessed by exterior passageways. Bàba and Uncle Bao disappeared into another building marked *Office* and appeared moments later waving room keys in the air. Ju and I squealed as we were handed our key, but we soon calmed ourselves after the disapproving looks we received from Māmā and Auntie Lian.

Once we had taken what we needed for

the night and put it in our rooms, we congregated in Năinai's and Yéyé's room where they had laid out a plethora of Chinese foods prepared and packed for this journey. We all tucked in as if we hadn't eaten for months, and soon only crumbs were left.

While our stomachs grumbled contentedly, we sat back and listened to Yéyé's stories from the past; his time as a boy growing up in the province of Fujian and his early adulthood before he travelled to Guangdong in search of a trade. There, of course, he had met and married Năinai.

"He was lucky that I said yes," Năinai laughed. "He won me over with his persistence!"

We had all heard these stories so many times that we could have retold them to the last detail, but none of us would have done them justice. Not really.

Yéyé told us about the Japanese occupation of his homeland and the struggles that this brought. He spoke of how this led to the beginning of World War 2 and the part that he had to play in his role as a fighter pilot. His eyes would glaze over as he shared with us his pride in his aircraft: a P-51 Mustang. It had been a brutal and scary time, but eventually the war had ended, and people had started to rebuild their lives again.

By this time, Ling had fallen asleep in my arms, so that was our cue to head to bed. Bàba carried my sister to Māmā's room, and Ju and I bid everyone a goodnight too.

Once we were tucked up under our blankets, Ju and I began happily chatting about how we thought Yéyé might have proposed. We had our western notions of flowers and serenades underneath window balconies, of course.

Ju declared that she believed Yéyé had taken Năinai to a restaurant for a romantic meal and then walked with her under the stars. She decided that he must have then gone down on one knee and popped the question whilst offering up an exquisite ring with the most beautiful jade center, which would have been surrounded by tiny diamonds.

"But Năinai wears no ring?" I said, confused.

"Well, maybe she is scared to lose it and has it locked up in a box somewhere safe," Ju said.

I shrugged, for I had no idea if this was the case, and we decided that we would ask Năinai the next day about what actually had happened.

A little while later, as Ju was telling me about a boy she liked at school, there came a light knocking at our door. We both froze, terrified that a stranger might be lurking outside.

"Mei, Ju, go to sleep! We can hear you chatting and giggling through the walls," said Uncle Bao from the other side of the door.

Ju threw her blanket over her head in horror, no doubt trying to figure out if her parents had heard her protestations of love — something that would *not* have been well received.

"Good night, Uncle Bao," I said as I tried to stifle a giggle. "We're turning our lights off now."

爱

We arrived in Washington D.C. in the late afternoon of the next day. Ju's relieved face as she got out of her car let me know that she hadn't been grilled about her love interest, so we could put that one down to luck. We needed to be more careful in future when we gossiped!

The hotel was simple but comfortable. This was where we would be staying for the next twelve nights, and it was fun unpacking all of our clothes and hanging them in the closet. Māmā and Ling were in the room to our left, and Uncle

Bao and Auntie Lian were in the room to our right. Bàba and Wing were farther down the hallway, and Nǎinai and Yéyé were in the room next to them.

Once we had all settled in, Uncle Bao knocked on our door to let us know that we were going out for dinner.

"*Oooh,*" I said. "I wonder which restaurant we will try tonight."

Ju laughed. "You know it'll be one in Chinatown, don't you? Can you see Yéyé sitting down to a Pizza Hut meal? He'd miss his rice too much!"

"I just think that if we are meant to be exploring American culture, then we should explore their food too? It's not that I don't love Chinese food, but it *would* be nice to have a taste of other different things sometimes too!"

"Hush, Mei! Nǎinai will scold you if she hears you talking like that!"

爱

As we all sat around the table in the Chinese restaurant we had discovered in Washington's Chinatown, I tried to keep a straight face as I looked at Ju's expression; her proposal bubble had been well and truly burst, and she was incredulous.

"No ring? Not even a little, simple one?" she asked our grandmother.

"No, Ju," said Nǎinai. "That is a western way, and we are Chinese!"

"But didn't you want a nice, sparkly ring to show off that you had got married?"

"Why on earth would we need that?" Nǎinai said. "It is custom for married women to wear their hair up, and this is our way of sharing with the world that we are no longer single."

"So, you didn't get any jewelry at all?" Ju persisted.

Auntie Lian decided to take charge of the conversation, as Nǎinai was looking more than a little perplexed by Ju.

"It's not the way it is done, gūniáng," she said. "In the western world, men propose to women with a ring. But Chinese custom dictates that the groom's family visits with the bride's and makes the formal proposal. They bring with them a great wedding gift of food, wine and jewelry as a way of thanking the family for raising their daughter so well."

"So the bride's *family* gets jewelry, but *she* doesn't?" Ju's eyebrows had now disappeared into her fringe as she tried to process this new information.

"Ju! Stop focusing on the jewelry," Năinai snapped. "Trinkets! That's all that is. The important message is the joining of the two families; a bond created out of respect and honor!"

"Sorry Năinai. But Māmā," Ju said as she turned back to look at Auntie Lian, "was it the same for you?"

"Yes, my child. However, your father did give me my special jade dragon statue, which is on the mantel at home. But no, I received no ring. Now, let that be an end to your obsession with western jewelry notions please."

As the adults resumed their conversations, Ju looked at me and rolled her eyes. "I'll make sure that *I* get a ring," she mouthed.

爱

For the rest of the vacation, we had fun exploring the monuments and museums that the city had to offer. Of course, one of the highlights was standing outside the White House—it was such an immense and imposing building, exuding power and prestige. We were also impressed with the Lincoln Memorial, and Wing was in awe as he gazed up at the colossal monument of the former American president.

We enjoyed plenty of picnics in the many green spaces of Washington, but our favorite was Rock Creek Park—the 1700 acres of lawns and woodlands made us feel as though we were in another world entirely. We even managed a few barbeques where we tried some American foods such as hotdogs and burgers. However, we still cooked them in honey rather than drench them in the typical American sauces.

During one of these barbeques, an American lady came up to me with a big smile on her face.

"Oh honey, I love your jacket. Is that one of your traditional pieces of clothing?"

She spoke really slowly and quite loudly, and I took a while to collect my thoughts. My shyness in front of strangers was quite crippling, and she had inadvertently piqued my anxiety about standing out when all I wanted to do was blend in. The only response I had was to bow my head and hide from her expectant gaze.

"Oh, poor thing. She doesn't understand you, Marge," said another lady—presumably her friend.

Ju came to my rescue.

"They are a traditional jacket of our culture, and they are really quite beautiful, don't you think?" she said as she showed off her own.

The woman looked surprised for a moment as she studied my cousin.

"Why, yes. I do think you are right, honey. The detail is so intricate and the colors are simply divine. Have you come over for a visit, dear? Your English is very good."

"Oh, no. We live here, don't we, Rose? Well, not in Washington, but in America."

All I could do was bob my head in agreement. I was sure the women had decided that I didn't have all my wits about me, and I felt like I had embarrassed myself once again. Why couldn't I have the confidence of Ju or even Ling? *They* never faltered when people spoke to them. But me? I froze. Every. Single. Time.

Ju grabbed my hand and started to pull me away, waving goodbye to the Americans as she went.

"You are silly," she said when we were out of earshot. "Why do you get so awkward around people?"

As I was about to reply, Ju ran off to where Auntie Lian was serving up the burgers. Clearly it had been a rhetorical question; my cousin knew me so well that she already knew the answer.

The most poignant moment of the trip came on the last day of the vacation when we visited The National Air and Space Museum. It had only opened a few years earlier, yet already it boasted an impressive assortment of aircraft. We all heard Yéyé's sharp intake of breath as we entered the World War 2 room.

Parked at an angle in one of the corners was a smallish khaki-green plane. It had a front propeller and a white star with an intersecting white line upon a blue circle printed upon its side. There were also large numbers situated just underneath the pilot's cockpit. It wasn't hard to work out why Yéyé was looking at it with such reverence.

"I never dreamed of seeing one of these again in my lifetime," he whispered as he ran his hand along the bodywork.

Then he leaned his forehead against the metal and closed his eyes. We could only imagine what memories, or nightmares, were playing in his mind. Năinai silently ushered us all away, leaving her husband to find the closure he needed from his past.

爱

Two days later, we pulled up, exhausted, outside our house. The car was still moving as I opened the passenger door, red plaid coat in hand.

"Mei, for goodness' sake! At least wait for Bàba to park!" scolded Māmā.

No sooner had the parking brake been applied than I was off, sprinting around the side of the house to find Ai. And there he was, lying in the shade of the green ash tree. My heart felt as though it would burst.

"Ai! Ai! I'm home!" I called as I ran to him.

My dog leapt up and bounded over to me, jumping up to lick my face over and over again.

Then his excitement overcame him, and he began to chase his tail as I looked on, laughing.

I sat down, leaning against the trunk of the tree, and Ai came over and flopped down next to me, his head resting in my lap as his eyes never strayed from my face. And so I spent the next couple of hours filling him in on all of the excitement of the vacation. Most importantly, I remembered to tell him many times exactly how much I had missed him while I had been away.

There we sat, enjoying each other's company, until Māmā knocked on the window to call me in for dinner. As I climbed the back steps, I turned to see the sun begin to dip below the neighboring rooftops, sending beautiful purple-tinged shades across the yard. I felt at peace; I was home.

自爱
Oh, to Be Chang'e!

Before I knew it, the time had come for me to start middle school. On the first morning of the fall semester, it felt like déjà vu as I hid once more under my blanket, willing the day not to begin. My bed creaked as someone sat down, their hand upon my covered shoulder.

"Oh jiějiě," whispered Ling, "are you feeling worried about today?"

I sighed and removed the blanket from my face. I gazed up into the solemn eyes of my sister and breathed in her essence, hoping it would steel me against what was to come.

"I am," I said. "I can't believe that Bethany, Faye and Filipa are all going to Bartholomew's, but I have to go by myself to Cuthbert Academy. I know that Bàba is convinced the teaching is better there, but ... Oh, mèimei!"

"What is it?"

My sister began to stroke my arm as her

face creased with worry. I felt guilty for burdening her with my problems, but it was nice to speak with someone who was able to voice a reply rather than simply console me with a lick of a slobbery tongue.

"You know how hard it is for me to make friends! Bàba wouldn't listen, though, and just said I would make more. But it's not that easy for me. I hate how awkward I am!"

"You are a bit," Ling said as she smiled at me, "but you must understand how great you are. You don't need to be awkward around people because you're lovely!"

"Am I?" I mumbled as Māmā came into the room to usher us up and out.

Ling gave my arm one more squeeze and skipped off to the bathroom to go and brush her teeth.

"Up!" Māmā said to me. "You'll make us late if you don't get a move on!"

"Yes, Māmā," I said as I silently begged the ground to open up and swallow me whole.

爱

Two hours later, I got off the bus outside the imposing, gray building which was to be my school for the next three years. I had spent the bus journey reminding myself of how this time wasn't going to be as bad as when I had started kindergarten; this time I would be able to understand my peers, and I had been signed up for school lunches too, so that was something at least.

But, the uneasiness in my stomach remained despite the effort I was making to calm myself. I knew no one here. There was no way to sugar-coat that fact. I was friendless once again, and as a socially-awkward child, who was already seen to be in the cultural minority, that was devastating. I tapped into every ounce of my courage, took a deep breath and stepped into my nightmare.

I found my classroom easily enough, and I hurried to an unoccupied desk at the back of the room. Hoping not to draw any attention to myself, I slid into the seat and then bowed my head to allow my curtain of hair to hide me from the world.

"Hi," said a voice right next to me and my breath hitched.

Was this someone attempting to make friends? With me? I lifted my head and saw that the girl who had spoken was sitting right next to me. There was no question about it; she was looking right at me. I smiled.

"Hi," I said. "I'm Rose."

"That's nice," said the girl. "But do you mind if my friend sits there? We always sit together."

"Oh ... *errrr* ... yes, of course," I mumbled as I felt the redness creep up my neck.

As I hurried out of the chair to remove myself from the embarrassing situation, I caught the strap of my bag on the corner of the desk. The desk toppled over and clattered to the floor, directing every pair of eyes in the classroom to my frantic efforts to pick it up again. The girl snickered and offered me no support. Of *course* she hadn't wanted to make friends with me. How stupid I was for thinking it!

As I righted the desk, I kept mumbling my apologies and willed the tears to stay away. That would be *too* humiliating on top of everything else.

I found another empty chair; this time at the front of the class. A boy sat at the desk next to it, reading a Marvel comic.

"Excuse me," I said, and the boy glanced up at me, his face remaining neutral. "Is it okay if I sit here?"

He looked me up and down, and then stared at me for a moment as he considered my request. Without uttering a word, he shrugged at me and returned his focus to his comic. Hoping that meant he wasn't bothered one way or another, I quickly slid into the chair just as the teacher came into the room.

爱

Invisible. In one day, I had become invisible.

All of my new peers had attended the lower school of Cuthbert Academy, so their friendship groups were established and impenetrable; they had no desire to welcome in the only Chinese girl in class, and they acted as though I wasn't even there. I spent my recess hiding in the farthest restroom stall, sitting on the closed toilet with my knees pulled up to my chest. I had never felt so alone.

To while away the time, I closed my eyes and imagined I was Chang'e, the beloved wife of Hou Yi, and I escaped into the oriental world of legend and cherry blossom.

I loved Chinese myths, and I spent much of my free time—when I wasn't with Ai—writing my own versions. My imagination was vivid, and stories flowed easily from me; words were never an issue when they graced the paper. This was a gift that I treasured, although I tended to keep it to myself—I had many a scribbling hidden in a battered box at the back of my closet.

As I remained in the stall, I thought that flying to the moon and watching the world from there, like Chang'e was reported to have done, would be far more preferable compared to where I was currently located. And I could only imagine how it would feel to be so unconditionally adored by another, and to be able to accept that adoration without question.

At lunchtime, I took my tray and found a table in the corner of the hall, hoping that I wouldn't be asked to move again. Eventually, the only spaces left were by me, so I bent my nose closer to my book to avoid any attention being drawn to me, my hair falling in its reliable curtains either side of my face.

"So, what's your name?" a girl asked as she sat next to me. "You're new here, aren't you?"

I looked up to see a pretty blond with a neat braid looking at me. I didn't recognize her from my class, but she looked to be a similar age to me.

"*Errrm* ... yes, I'm new. My name is M—*errr* ... Rose."

"I thought I hadn't seen you before. I

would have remembered. My name is Kendal. Which class are you in?"

"6C."

"*Ahh*. That would explain it. I'm in 6A. You speak very good English. Where are you from?"

"I'm ... *errr* ... from here," I said.

"Really? But, you look Chinese?"

"I am Chinese, but ... *errrm* ... I was born here, so I guess I'm American too," I said, hoping to move off the subject that I was still trying to sort out in my own head.

"How can you be American *and* Chinese?" said Kendal.

"I'm still figuring it out," I mumbled. "Tell me about you."

I had said the right thing because that was clearly Kendal's favorite topic of conversation. The remainder of the lunch period was spent with her sharing every detail of her privileged life, but I didn't mind; to the outside world, I was no longer a friendless nobody.

爱

When I got home from school, I quickly popped out to see Ai before I did my homework and my chores. Lying in the shade under the green ash tree, he didn't seem to hear my approach. I noted now how his body had thickened out over the last couple of years, and there was also a plentiful smattering of gray around his muzzle. My old friend was slowing down, and this made me so sad.

Sitting down next to him and making as little noise as I could manage—I didn't want to startle him when he was sleeping so soundly—I became mesmerized by the rise and fall of his chest. It helped to regulate my own breathing, and I found it incredibly relaxing. His gruff little snores were endearing, and I thanked my lucky stars that this treasured soul had found us all of those years ago. He was my rock.

I leaned back against the tree trunk and closed my eyes, relishing in the bird song from above and the gentle breeze upon my face. After a while, I noticed that Ai's snores had stopped, so I opened my eyes and looked down to find him gazing up at me. The moment our eyes met, his tail began to thump on the ground.

"Oh, Ai. Let me tell you about my day ..."

And Ai rested his head on my lap, ready for me to begin.

爱

During our game of Mahjong that evening, Bàba noticed that I was quieter than usual.

"Do you not like your new school?" he said to me.

"I'm still getting used to it, Bàba," I said. "I'm sure that I'll like it really soon."

"Have you made any friends?" asked Māmā.

"Yes. Her name is Kendal, and she said she will introduce me to all of her friends tomorrow."

Wing looked at me whilst Māmā nodded in approval; he had noted the flat tone in my voice that my mother had missed.

"You okay?" he mouthed to me, and I nodded as I gave him a sad smile.

The game of Mahjong continued. I had been designated as East Wind, and so I discarded the extra tile that I didn't want and said its name.

"Eight Circle."

I was beginning to get the hang of the game now, but I still wasn't as proficient as Wing—he won most hands nowadays, even beating Bàba. No one wanted my tile, and play moved around to my mother. She picked up a

The Origami Balloon

face-down tile from the center of the table, studied it and then discarded it again.

"Three Bamboo," she said.

"Oh! Pong!" I said, happy to have made a meld, and I laid my tiles flat on the table to prove it to my opponents.

"Did you hear about the Zhao boy?" my father said to my mother.

"Yes, Mrs. Huang told me the other day. Silly boy has ruined his life!" she said, pursing her lips in disapproval.

"What did he do, Bàba?" said Wing.

"He was caught stealing from people's houses along with two of his American friends. They are all going to court to be charged for theft. They stole a pretty penny by all accounts!" my father replied.

To read between the lines, it was clear from the way that our father looked at each of us in turn that we would be ostracized if ever we brought such shame upon our family name. Zhao Zhang Wei was seventeen, and it had been said for a while now that he'd gone off the rails a bit; rebelling against the strictness of his upbringing, no doubt. But in doing so, he had made a bad choice, and now he was being punished for it. He would be lucky if his family ever spoke to him again. It was also very clear who my parents blamed for influencing Zhao Zhang Wei's lawless behavior.

"Speaking of pretty pennies," my father continued, "Li Hao let me know that the Dow Jones has risen in the market again. It may be time to look at more investments."

As the talk of money and investment continued, I zoned out and ruminated over my new friendship with Kendal. It was true that we didn't really have anything in common, but she was confident and liked to talk, so I thought she might balance me out quite well. If anything, she might be my way of surviving the next few years of school; from the little time that I had spent with her, it was clear that people seemed to like her, so that meant they would probably accept me more readily if I was associated with her.

"I'm calling!" said Wing, arranging his tiles on the table so that we could see he had all of his melds and was just waiting for his pair.

"I'm calling too," said Bàba, grinning at my brother.

"Five Bamboo," said Māmā.

"Mahjong!" yelled Wing, beaming at us all.

自爱
Bunty's Cookies and Cakes

Once I started 8th grade, my parents decided that it was time for me to get a Saturday job.

"But who should I ask, Bàba?"

"Use your initiative, gūniáng! But, if you don't find a job by the end of the week, I'll find you a job with me in the restaurant. It'll probably be washing pots, but we all have to start somewhere."

And so my job hunting began. It wasn't that I wanted to avoid spending time with Bàba, but rather that I wanted to see if I *could* find a job on my own. That would be a huge thing to achieve for me—it meant that I would have to force my way through my own inhibitions. It would also make my parents proud of me.

Every day that week after school, I walked the streets around the district, asking for jobs in delis, cafes and even Laundromats. No one was hiring, but I persevered.

On Friday, I came across a little bakery, tucked down a side street called *Bunty's Cookies and Cakes*. It looked a little shabby from the outside, but when I pushed opened the door, I was greeted by a merry tinkling sound from a little brass door bell that made me want to smile.

Heavenly aromas permeated the cozy little space, and I could see seven circular tables, each covered with a different color of gingham cloth. Upon the cloth, in the center of every table, was a little vase with a small arrangement of freshly cut flowers. They were so pretty, and they really helped to make the interior homely. Several people sat at these tables, but they were so engrossed in their own conversations that they paid me no attention.

My eyes traveled to the far end of the shop where the sales counter was. Upon it, within glass-topped cake domes, were all kinds of sugary treats, and I gravitated towards them as I took note of the many different sprinkles and toppings. My mouth began to water as the vision in front of me, coupled with the many delicious smells, assailed me.

A crash came from the little kitchen beyond, which I could just see through a service hatch in the wall.

"Oh bother!" said a voice.

"*Errrm* ... are ... are you okay?" I called through.

"Oh, yes dear," said an older lady as she came bustling through to the counter, balancing a tray of brownies on her arm. "I'm so sorry. I didn't hear you come in! I just dropped the other tray of brownies on the floor. How very clumsy of me!"

Would you like me to help you to clear them up?" I said.

The lady stopped fussing with the tray on her arm and looked at me over her half-moon glasses. With her gray curls and rosy cheeks, she reminded me of a quintessential American granny. She also oozed kindness, and I felt instantly comfortable in her company.

"Well, now. Isn't that a sweet thing to offer, dear," she said, smiling at me.

"I don't mind, honestly," I said. "I can have it brushed up for you in no time! I'm Rose, by the way."

"It's nice to meet you, Rose. I'm Bunty. Now how can *I* help *you*?"

"I—I ... *errr* ... was wondering if ... *errmm* ... you—"

"Speak up, dear. I can't help you if I can't hear you," Bunty chuckled.

The Origami Balloon

I took a deep breath, met her gaze and said, "I was wondering if you might have a job for me? My parents have told me that I must get a Saturday job, so I was hoping that you might have one to offer me?"

"*Ahhh*, I see. Well now. How old are you?"

"I'm 13, although I'll be 14 in four months time," I said.

"And what experience do you have?"

"I bake all the time with my mother, and I help around the house every day doing my chores. I'm hard-working and honest, and I won't let you down."

Bunty stared at me for several moments, and I started to feel the dusky blush creep up my neck and begin to warm my cheeks. I dipped my head, feeling that I had, yet again, made a complete fool of myself.

"So, would you like to start tomorrow? I can give you a month's trial and then we'll see. What do you think?"

"Oh, thank you so much! Thank you!"

Bunty laughed and said, "Don't thank me yet! You've got to earn the job first!"

"Oh I will, you'll see," I promised, and with that I hurried through to the kitchen and began to sweep up the broken brownies that were scattered on the floor while Bunty leaned against the doorframe watching me.

Once I got home, I ran around to the back yard to tell Ai my good news. Upon hearing my calls, he came hobbling out of his kennel to greet me. I threw my arms around his neck and hugged him tight, telling him how excited I was to have found a perfect little job in the bakery.

"And she seems so kind, Ai." I said as we sat together under the green ash tree. "She says I must be there at 7 a.m. tomorrow morning so that I can help her to bake the cakes for opening at 9 a.m. Māmā and Bàba are going to be so proud of me!"

Ai wagged his tail and looked up into my eyes. My heart sank a little as I saw the cloudiness in his right eye, and there was *so* much gray around his muzzle now. I took his face in my hands and gazed into his eyes, hoping that he would read the depth of my love for him in my own and that this would help to engrave it on his loyal heart.

"I love you so much, Ai. How are you, boy? Are you in much pain?"

Ai simply wagged his tail and licked my hand, so I dropped a kiss upon his nose and let him rest his head back in my lap again. He settled down immediately and closed his eyes, so I began to hum the little Chinese nursery rhyme,

Xīng Xīng Duō, Wá Wa Duō, whilst absently stroking his fur.

Once Ai began to snore, I took great care when sliding out from under his head so not to wake him. Giving him one last kiss upon his muzzle, I hurried into the house to share the good news of my job with my family and to complete my homework and chores.

爱

I came to love my job at the bakery. Bunty, who insisted that I called her Auntie Bunty, was the loveliest boss, and I learned so many new skills that I could then bring home and share with Māmā.

Even though the bakery was situated on a quiet side street, it was busy from the moment we opened the doors until we locked them again at 5 p.m. Auntie Bunty's baking reputation spread for miles around, it would seem.

Dealing with the cash register helped my mental math beyond belief, and I was soon working out the calculations in my head without the need for the calculator. The regulars became used to my awkward shyness, playfully teasing me for it when they visited.

"Gentle Rose," they would say. "But surely you have some thorns hidden there somewhere?"

"Leave her alone," Bunty would swat at them like flies. "There's nothing thorny about my Rose. She's as sweet as they come!"

And then they would laugh as the compliment made me blush even more than the teasing.

At school, I survived each day by keeping to Kendal's shadow. There was never any expectation for me to talk, as my friend did enough of that for both of us. And when someone did ask me a question, Kendal would typically answer it for me. I never really minded though, as I was still paralyzed with fear every time anyone paid me even the smallest amount of attention.

"So, I'm going to the mall on Saturday," said Sophie one lunchtime. "Do you all want to come?"

"*Ooooh*, yes. My mom has given me some money to buy a new top, so you can all help me to pick one out," said Kendal, her face lighting up at the thought of treating herself. "And you'll come too, won't you, Rose?"

"I—I … *errrr* … can't," I muttered. "I'll be at work."

"At work?" Kendal laughed. "What do you mean you'll be at work?"

I hadn't yet told my friends about my Saturday job, as I knew they wouldn't understand. None of them had to earn their own funds, but my parents didn't believe in the concept of an allowance.

"Has your dad got you working in his Chinese restaurant?" Katie said, and she laughed as though it were the funniest thing in the world.

"No, I—I work in a bakery just off from Third Avenue," I mumbled, wishing the subject would change onto something else. "What top would you like to buy?" I said, trying to bring the conversation back to Kendal. No such luck.

"How long have you been working *there* for?" demanded Kendal, and the look in her eyes let me know that she wasn't impressed that I hadn't already told her.

"Oh, *errrm* ... about three months now," I said. "It's my parents' way of teaching me the value of money by getting me to make my own. If I want to buy anything for myself, I have to save up for it."

"Why on earth would you want to do that?" laughed Katie. "That sounds *so* boring! If I want anything, I just ask Pop for it! You need to start learning how to use puppy-eyes to get your way!"

I smiled an awkward smile and looked down again at my hands.

"Oh well," said Sophie. "The rest of us can meet at the main entrance on Saturday. Say about 10 a.m.?"

爱

I was out of favor with Kendal after that; she made it quite clear to me that she hadn't appreciated finding out about my job at the same time as everyone else.

So the remaining months of middle school were lonely ones. Every recess, I found myself hiding again in the farthest stall of the restroom. Now I spent the time in there writing my own stories, inventing worlds that made more sense to me than the one I had to try and exist in every day, and creating characters who accepted me as I was.

Some days I fought dragons on the tops of the craggiest mountains, rescuing people who were in trouble; other days I swam with the mermaids in the sea, marveling at the underwater wonders that were usually hidden from human sight. In each story that I wrote, I heard my voice sing loud and clear from every page.

One of the stories that I wrote whilst hiding in the stall soon became a firm favorite of mine. It was about Ai, a warrior hound, who had the biggest heart of gold. Resilient and loyal, his integrity was a shining beacon for everyone in the world who wished to be good and true. A growl from him was usually enough to make the dishonest quiver in fear and decide upon a new, more righteous path in life.

Ai was a sage; a master of all, who helped people to see the beauty in life, but he also made sure that they saw the beauty within themselves too. After all, my Ai loved me as *I* was, despite my idiosyncrasies.

At the end of every recess, I would pack my writing back into its folder and stuff it into my bag, ready for the next opportunity to allow my mind to explore more fantastical places once again.

My poor social standing was further hindered by the fact that Māmā took me to the orthodontist just after Christmas of 8th grade. She had decided that I needed help to straighten my teeth. So, big metal brackets were secured to each tooth, upper and lower, and then thin, metal wires were connected to pull the teeth into line. I looked like I had a train track in my mouth, which meant that I was even less willing to smile now than I had been before. And the teasing I got at school for it was constant and cruel.

"*Oi*, metal mouth! Make sure you don't get food stuck in your wires!"

"Can I catch the 3:10 to Naperville, please? Oh sorry! My mistake!"

And so it went on. And as if that wasn't enough to bring the bullies down on me, a flurry of hormones just after my fourteenth birthday meant that my face broke out in pimples. No matter which lotions I tried, none seemed to take away the redness of my face or ease the outbreaks. Even Māmā's many herbal concoctions drew a blank.

Unfortunately, this gave Kendal the perfect opportunity to get her own back on me by humiliating me in front of everyone just before 8th grade ended.

"*Ewwww*. Look at you. You're grotesque, with your mouth full of metal and a dot-to-dot puzzle on your face!" she said, looking around to make sure that her audience was laughing along. "And to think that I felt *sorry* for you when I first saw you. But I made the right choice in the end by throwing the ugly stray back out onto the street where she belongs! Didn't I, girls?"

I couldn't see Kendal or her pack of hyenas through the tears that were welling up in my eyes, and I ran off down the hallway to the echoing laughs of my peers bouncing off the walls behind me. I crashed through the door of my sanctuary and quickly locked it behind me, pulling my knees up to my chest and hugging them to me.

I stayed there for the rest of the afternoon, skipping my classes. Then just before the end-of-day bell rang, I silently hastened down the empty hallway and out onto the sunny street.

I needed my rock. I needed my Ai. He knew me and loved me regardless of horrid pimples or unsightly metal in my mouth. He didn't care if I was Chinese in a western world or an American in a Chinese world. He saw to the very core of me, and he had decided from day one that I was worth loving just as I was. So why did others find that so hard to do?

I rushed around the side of the house, my tears still blinding me. Flinging myself down onto my knees, I crawled into the kennel where I could just about see Ai stretched out in the shadows of the far corner. Sniffing and wiping my nose on my sleeve, I made my way to him as quickly as I could so that I could soak up his love and acceptance.

But, something was wrong.

My hands eagerly reached for him to pull him into a hug, but my loyal companion didn't respond.

"Ai! Ai! It's me! Wake up, wake up!" I began to sob as I shook him, trying to ignore the dawning truth. "Ai! I need you! You can't leave me! I love you! Ai!"

But Ai had gone. His wise eyes were now unseeing, and his comforting body was cold and stiff. I buried my face in his fur and wept and wept as my heart shattered into a million pieces.

And so it was here that Bàba found me hours later. He guided me back into the house and gave me some strong tea to settle me down, but I was barely responsive. I felt as though I was at one end of a very long tunnel, and my family was at the other end … distant and unreachable in my grief. They even sounded far away when they spoke to me, though the rational part of my brain knew that they were only inches away.

"I'll make her some soup," Māmā said. "She's had a nasty shock."

But the soup remained untouched, unwanted. There was only one thing that I needed in that moment, and he was gone.

My father carried me to bed that night, and when he had left the room, I felt Ling crawl in behind me, tuck herself under my blankets and wrap her arms around me.

"I'm so sorry, jiějiě," she whispered into my hair. "He was a good boy ... the best."

But no matter how much I wanted to answer Ling, I couldn't. I couldn't form the words because there *were* no words precious enough to describe what Ai had meant to me. He had been my guiding light, my compass, my linchpin. He had been all of those, and yet he had been so much more. But now ... I closed my eyes as I tried to force from my mind what I knew to be true.

Ling sighed and snuggled closer into my back as she settled down to sleep. I was so grateful for the warmth her company gave me, and soon my exhausted mind shut down, and I, too, slept.

爱

We buried Ai the next day as the muted rays of dawn crept over the rooftops. We placed him in the ground under the canopy of the green ash tree and laid a posy of freshly picked daisies upon his grave. My chest now felt hollow and, as I gazed down upon my faithful friend's final resting place, I prayed that he was safe and well, frolicking happily on the ridge beyond Rainbow Bridge.

"I'll see you again one day, Ai. Keep looking out for me, and meet me when I come. I love you," I whispered to the skies as the first of the day's raindrops fell to mix with the tears upon my face.

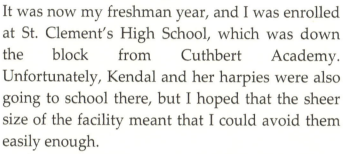

自爱
Life after Ai

It was now my freshman year, and I was enrolled at St. Clement's High School, which was down the block from Cuthbert Academy. Unfortunately, Kendal and her harpies were also going to school there, but I hoped that the sheer size of the facility meant that I could avoid them easily enough.

Since losing Ai three months previously, I had merely existed through every day. I couldn't seem to find joy in anything, and every chore that I had to complete was carried out on auto-pilot. I had become an elective mute, and most people gave me a wide berth to avoid the awkwardness in having to deal with me. Even when I went to work at the bakery on Saturdays, Auntie Bunty (despite her warmth and kindness) couldn't penetrate the fog in my mind, and eventually she assigned me to kitchen duties to keep me away from the customers. To her credit, any other boss would have fired me by then for my lack of interaction.

It wasn't solely the loss of Ai that had led to this broken version of me, although that *had* been the final blow to shatter my fragile self. No ... I had been falling into a pit of confusion and self-loathing for so long, and Ai had been my lifeline; my anchor. He had been the one to keep me tethered to the belief that I was worth loving, and now that he was gone, there was nothing to stop me from falling deeper and deeper into that well of despair.

I knew that my family loved me, but their love came with so many conditions and expectations, which I was always so anxious to meet. Ai had loved me unconditionally, without judgment. I was never found to be wanting in his eyes.

I remembered back to the time when my world had made sense—playing hide and seek in Nǎinai's and Yéyé's garden; watching little Ling chasing butterflies in the park and feeding steamed buns to the ducks, or not; our weekly trips to the museum when we were still being home-schooled. Now, I felt so naïve to have hoped for those days to have gone on forever.

From the moment I had become Rose, my experiences had only added to the negative voices in my head.

"Who are *you* to try and be American, Rose? You don't even *look* American!"

"Why do you always dress like you're going to church? And that food you eat!"

"You should be proud to be Chinese, gūniáng! We have our ways and they have theirs! Remember that!"

From the moment I had been given my western name, I had felt as though my identity had been torn in two, and both halves were being battered by the strong winds of insecurity, misunderstanding and judgment, becoming tattered around the edges and more worn as the years passed by.

I pushed open the back door to look down upon the rose bush that I had planted to mark Ai's grave. The huge blooms were a deep violet, and I had chosen that particular species because it was called *Blue without You*. It had seemed most fitting.

Bàba had taken down the old kennel; there wouldn't be another dog for the Lee family, and my father had decided that its presence wasn't helping me to get past the loss of my loyal pet. But, the flaking panels were still stacked against the fence, waiting to be taken to the garbage dump. I closed my eyes to conjure up memories of the many moments that I had spent snuggled

The Origami Balloon

up in that space with my best friend. A dull ache thudded in my chest, and I embraced the misery.

"Mei! Come in and help with breakfast," said Māmā from the kitchen behind me.

I sighed and half-turned to comply when something by the rose bush caught my eye. Tangled up in the thorns was a golden cord, at the end of which floated a beautiful, golden, heart-shaped balloon. It bobbed around in the breeze, and I gasped aloud, wondering where it could have come from.

I rushed down the steps to go and untangle it, worrying that the lower branches of the green ash tree would burst it; it was far too pretty a balloon for me to allow that to happen! As I got closer, I could see that this was unlike any other balloon I'd ever seen: it looked as though it were made from origami. How was that even possible?

Suddenly, a brisk gust of wind loosened the thorns' hold on the cord by tugging on the balloon, and it floated up and out of reach.

"Gūniáng! What are you doing out there?" Māmā called from the back door. "I asked you to come and help with breakfast. Don't make me ask for a third time!"

"Sorry, Māmā," I said. "I was trying to rescue the balloon, but the wind freed it."

Becoming Mei-Rose

"Balloon? What balloon?" Māmā said, frowning at me.

"Why, that one," I said, pointing to the heart-shaped balloon, which was now bobbing just above the canopy of the green ash tree.

"Are you feeling unwell? There is no balloon there! Do you need me to make you some soup? Maybe you have a fever. Come here so that I can check your forehead."

"No, I am fine, Māmā," I said, now completely baffled, as I could still see the balloon as clear as day. "Can you really not see it?"

"No, gūniáng! There is no balloon there. Now come here so I can take a look at you."

Gazing once more at the golden delight still bobbing in the same place, I sighed and trudged back to my mother, who wore an expression of concern mixed with exasperation. Upon deeming me to be fit and healthy, she chided me for the worry I had caused her.

"You and your imagination, Mei! You'll have people start to say you are poorly in the head. Now, come on! There is breakfast to make and school to get to. Lái!"

The bus dropped me off an hour later on Fourth Avenue, which was a 10-minute walk from St. Clement's High School. I was still pondering the strange moment from earlier when I heard an excited voice call my name.

"Rose? Rose Lee? Is that you?"

I stopped in my tracks and turned around to see my old friend Filipa running up to me with a huge smile.

"I knew it had to be you! No one else walks like you do," she laughed as she threw her arms around me.

I raised my hand to cover my mouth as I said, "But why are you here?"

"I'm going to St. Clement's! Don't tell me that you are too? Oh, that would be so amazing! I have missed you so much!"

Filipa linked her arm through mine as we continued to walk, and she began filling me in on all of her news since I had last seen her. She didn't seem to notice my acne or my clumsy attempts to hide my braces when I spoke; she just seemed genuinely happy to see me.

I told her all about my awful time at middle school, and she gave my arm a squeeze. When I told her about Ai, she stopped walking and turned to give me the biggest hug.

"Oh, that makes me so sad," she said. "I

remember how much you loved that dog. And don't worry about Miss Prissy-Panties! You've got me now, and I'm going nowhere!"

Once we had found our classroom, Filipa made a beeline for two empty desks that were next to each other.

"Here we go," she said as she sat at one and indicated for me to sit at the other. "What is it? You've gone pale!"

"Over there," I whispered with my head bent, "coming through the door. It's the girl I was telling you about and her friends."

I peeked sideways to see Kendal sashaying her way over to me, taking in the measure of Filipa as she came.

"Oh look who we have here!" she sneered. "I see you've found another little waif and stray."

"Excuse me? *What* did you just call me?" said Filipa as she stood up and faced the bully.

Kendal, unused to people confronting her, took a step back and put her hands up as if to fend Filipa off. "Easy, tiger, or I may need to put you back in your cage!"

Filipa looked enraged as she pushed her desk to one side and stepped towards Kendal. I had never seen this side to my friend during our time in elementary school, so I watched with open curiosity.

"Speak to me, or Rose, like that again, and I'll put you in your place! Remember that, criança mimada!"

Unsure as to the name that Filipa had just called her, Kendal glared as us for a moment longer before spinning on her heel and flicking her ponytail at us. She then stalked down to the desks at the front that had been clearly earmarked for her and her posse.

Looking very smug, Filipa straightened her desk and sat back down. "I'll be surprised if she bothers us again. I think she just peed a little in her panties!"

We both burst out laughing as the teacher came into the room. For the first time in such a long time, I felt as though I wasn't alone.

爱

That lunchtime, Filipa and I went into the huge canteen to suss out the territory. We could see that different areas seemed to be allocated to freshmen, sophomores, juniors and seniors, and then, within each area, there were further subdivisions of jocks, cheerleaders, geeks and so on. It was time to stake our place in our new school.

After scanning the room, Filipa finally pointed to a small area at the back of the hall. Congregated there were lots of teenagers of all ages who were chatting and laughing. As we got nearer, we could hear music playing on a stereo next to a group of older boys, and a couple of them were performing some impressive dance moves. There was so much energy emanating from this group, and what had made Filipa point it out in the first place was the fact that it was comprised of many different nationalities.

"Hi," Filipa said to a freckled-faced girl with raven-black curly hair. "I'm Filipa, and this is my friend, Rose. Is it okay if we have our lunch with you?"

"Sure, of course! I'm Sinead," the girl replied in a thick, Irish accent. "Tom, Angela, Rhys, move over!" She jostled against the group of girls and boys next to her on the seat. "We have new friends joining us."

And so we had found our tribe; many of them second generation children—born in America yet of first generation immigrants who had come to the United States seeking better job opportunities and new adventures. I was hoping that maybe, just maybe, they too might understand the confusion of having dual heritages and trying to identify as both.

爱

Filipa caught the same bus home as me, although she was getting off two stops earlier. I felt so content as I looked out of the window at the world trundling by. This had been a good day — the first in a long time.

All of a sudden, I sat up straight and grabbed Filipa's arm.

"Well, would you look at that?" I said in disbelief.

"What?" said Filipa, craning her neck to see past me and to where I was pointing.

"There! I don't believe it! It's the balloon again!"

"*Ooooh*, a balloon? I love balloons! Where is it?"

I dropped my hand and turned to look at my friend, who continued to search the skies beyond the window. I remembered my mother's reaction that morning as I had pointed it out to her too. And now, as vividly as the hand in front of my face, I could see the golden origami balloon floating along in the sky behind the bus, but Filipa couldn't. That much was clear. And my mother hadn't seen it this morning either.

I rubbed my eyes and squinted through the window again. Yes, it was definitely there, yet there was no possible explanation for why it seemed to be following us. Or why no one else could see it.

"Oh, sorry! It was just a plastic bag. My mistake!" I said to a disappointed Filipa, who just laughed as I continued to watch the balloon bob along high up in the sky beside us.

"Maybe you need to get your eyes checked!"

And, as I discovered when I got home, she wasn't the only one to think that. My mother declared, as soon as I entered the house, that she had made an appointment for me at the eye doctor later that afternoon.

"We haven't had your eyes checked for years, and with you seeing things this morning, I think that now is the time to remedy that!"

As if braces and acne wasn't enough, two days later I arrived at school with over-large, round black glasses that my mother had chosen for me. Personally, I would have preferred a bag to wear over my head, as that would have shielded me from the stares and snickers that were sent my way from the jocks and their girlfriends. I don't think that I could have felt any uglier than I did right then, and just when I had started feeling better about getting out of bed in the mornings.

Filipa, on the other hand, was blossoming. Not that she would have ever wanted me to compare myself to her, but she was undeniably gorgeous. Long, wavy, brown hair and a body that had already hit puberty, she caught many a boy's eye. She never flaunted it, but she caught those glances and appreciated them. I envied her grace and her confidence, her control and her style. I had none of those qualities, and it was becoming more and more obvious the older I became. I was floundering, and I felt like the ugly duckling that had no hope of turning into the beautiful swan.

The following Saturday, I locked up the bakery with Auntie Bunty after another busy day.

"Why on earth would you let your mother choose those awful glasses for you, Rose?" Auntie Bunty said as she tutted at me. "I can see how miserable they make you. And you're such a dainty thing that they are far too big for your face!"

"Have *you* tried saying no to my mother?" I sighed.

Auntie Bunty shook her head and tutted once more before waving goodbye to me. I continued onto Third Avenue, gazing absentmindedly into the shop windows that I passed as I walked toward the bus stop.

As I passed Waldenbooks, I stopped dead in my tracks only to have an angry businessman collide into the back of me on the busy street.

"What do you think you're playing at? You need to get back to Chinatown if you can't be trusted on our streets!"

"Oh, I'm sorry!" I called after him, but he seemed not to hear; or maybe not to care.

I stayed rooted to the spot, though, as I gazed at the sight that had caused this drama. Clearly the issue hadn't really been with my eyes, as there, in the top right-hand corner of the shop's large window, I could see the reflection of a shiny heart-shaped balloon bobbing in the air as though suspended.

I turned slowly on the spot, careful not to bump into anyone else and ... yes, sure enough, there it was on the other side of the street, just hovering in the air. No one was paying it any attention, so I could only fathom that this balloon was here for me alone, yet I had no idea why.

I decided to start walking again, and I kept checking over my shoulder to see the balloon now moving, following me down the street. I took a detour down a side street, and I started to run, feeling more than a little anxious that this was happening. The balloon kept up with me, albeit keeping the same distance between us.

I rounded the corner of the next street and then stopped to peek back around the edge of the shop. The balloon halted in the air. I ducked back around the corner and pressed my back against the wall of the building. My stomach was churning and I was starting to feel a little scared, but then I felt a strange tug in my chest. I peeked around the corner again, but as I couldn't see the balloon, I exhaled slowly, trying to calm my nerves.

However, a moment later I saw a glint of gold coming from a doorway farther down the street before it disappeared once more. All the fear that I had felt dissipated in that moment as I laughed out loud. The balloon seemed to be imitating my weird game of hide and seek! There it was again, peeking around the doorway before hiding once more.

I noticed the strange tug again in my chest; a dull ache that had lingered there for far too long now but which I had grown used to. The balloon seemed to be reminding me of it.

I began retracing my steps back along the street towards the doorway where the balloon was hiding, but out it popped and floated away again to the same distance it had kept from me earlier. I stopped. It stopped. I changed direction ... and so did it. I was beginning to feel like I had fallen down the proverbial rabbit hole; either that, or I was losing my mind.

Having wasted enough time chasing a supposedly imaginary balloon, I quickly made my way to the bus stop. I knew Māmā would worry if I wasn't home soon, and then I would be berated; it wouldn't do to miss our game of Mahjong.

爱

That evening, Ling and I helped Māmā to make the Kung Pao shrimp for dinner. Our mother had already marinated the shrimp in rice wine and cornstarch while we had been at school, and she'd even prepared the sauce, which meant that we just had to prepare the vegetables and cook it all up in the huge wok.

While I measured out the other ingredients, Ling began chopping the fresh chili. She was chattering away to me and Māmā about the science class she had enjoyed earlier in the day, and she foolishly forgot what ingredient she was dealing with.

"*Aiiiiii-ya*! *Ouch*!! Oh, Māmā!" she cried as

I looked up to see what the commotion was about.

Her eyes were streaming, and it was clear that she had rubbed them with her chili hands. I think we had all learned that lesson the hard way, but I felt bad for my little sister as Māmā ushered her out of the room and to the bathroom where she could rinse out her eyes.

So, chopping up the remaining chili peppers and the scallions, I then set about slicing up the garlic cloves and fresh ginger. After that, I began to roast the peanuts in the empty wok until they were lightly brown before transferring them to a bowl. Next, I popped in some oil and mixed in the remaining ingredients, stirring them until the shrimp started to curl up and turn pink. I had made this meal a million times, so I was confident in continuing without Māmā's guidance.

Finally, I added the sauce to the wok and stirred it until it all began to simmer. The kitchen was full of the most incredible aromas, and Wing came in to set the table. Once he had completed his task, I added the roasted peanuts to the wok and gave it all a quick stir before bringing the wok to the table.

Whilst I did that, Wing came over to drain the plain rice and put it into a bowl, ready to serve alongside the Kung Pao shrimp. He then called our family to the table so that we could all give thanks for our food and tuck in.

Whilst we were eating, I decided to find the courage to ask Māmā about my glasses.

"I was wondering if it was possible to choose another pair of glasses … please?"

"Can you not see through those?"

"Yes, Māmā, but they are so big for my face that people are laughing at me."

"*Humph*. You shouldn't care so much what people say or do. What do they know?"

"Please, Māmā?"

"I spent good money on those, Mei. If you want another pair of glasses, then you will have to pay for them out of your own money."

"Oh, thank you! I will. Wing, Ling," I said, turning to my siblings. "Will you help me to choose some new ones?"

And so I had taken the first step in trying to feel happier about how I looked. My brother and sister were going to come with me after school on Monday to find a pair that suited my small face, and I couldn't wait.

As I got ready for bed that night, I remembered the balloon. I knelt on my bed and opened the curtains to look out upon the moonlit back yard. I was expecting to see it now, so it came as no surprise to see the golden heart, half in the shadows, floating gently up and down above Ai's rose bush. Ai. My beautiful Ai.

As I watched the balloon, I found my breathing begin to follow its movements; as it floated up, I breathed in, and as it floated down, I breathed out. Up and down; in and out.

"What are you looking at, jiějiě?" said Ling as she came into the room having brushed her teeth.

"Oh … nothing, really, mèimei," I said as I turned to my sister and smiled. I noted that her eyes were still a little red from the chili. "I'm just imagining a message from Ai, I think."

Ling gave me a hug before she jumped into her bed, and I turned off the light. I got into my own bed and lay down facing the window, gazing up at the moon above.

"Night, Ai," I whispered into my pillow as I closed my eyes, a smile upon my lips, and soon I was fast asleep.

自爱
A Soup for Every Occasion

Just after my fifteenth birthday, I was convinced that I was dying. I'd had an ache in my stomach for several days, and then I went to the bathroom and made a most unpleasant discovery.

"Māmā! Māmā!" I yelled as I stared wide-eyed at the tissue in my hand.

Māmā came bustling into the room; a look of panic crossed her face as she registered the expression on mine.

"What is it, gūniáng? What is the emergency?"

And then her eyes alighted on the tissue that I was still clasping in my hand.

"*Aii-ya*, Mei! You had me worried!" she chuckled.

My mouth agape, I stared at my mother as I tried to fathom how this traumatic situation was not fazing her. Her eldest daughter was bleeding to death, and she was standing there chuckling at me.

"Ah, your face! It's only your *monthlies*," she said, although she whispered the last word, indicating to me that it was a little distasteful.

Still incredulous, I watched as my mother then started rummaging in the bathroom cabinet before pulling out a little package and thrusting it at me. I just stared at it, so Māmā proceeded to make little jabbing motions with it, indicating that I should take it.

"What do I do with that?" I said.

"Put it *down there* ... and then change it for another one when it gets *dirty*," she said, now looking a little uncomfortable. "I'll go and make you some soup."

Soup. That was Māmā's answer to every malady. Whether we had a fever, a stomach ache or a fright, there was always a traditional Chinese medicinal herb or two that could be added to soup.

So when I eventually went downstairs, feeling as though I was back in diapers, my mother presented me with a steaming cup of herbal soup.

"Dang gui and ginger," she said, nodding her head. "This will help with the cramps."

And that was it. That was my introduction

to the terrifying world of menstrual cycles. Filipa laughed when I told her about it the next day at school.

"Oh no … that is too funny! Stop it," she giggled as I recounted my absolute horror regarding the whole situation, over-emphasizing my mother's whisperings of the awkward words. "I started mine when I was 11, so I just assumed that you'd started yours too! If I'd known, I would have given you the heads up!"

So, periods and pimples. They were the only indicators that I had hit puberty. No other changes to my body that would have helped me to view myself more favorably. Where were the curves that were so appealing? *My* body just resembled that of a skinny beanpole, and it didn't go unnoticed by the bullies on the school bus. They drew pictures of me on the fogged-up windows: a train track instead of a mouth, glasses … and inverted breasts. Apparently mine were so small that they were in danger of popping out of my back. Hilarious.

Filipa would always yell at the bullies and wipe off the pictures, but the images remained imprinted on my brain. I felt like I was a laughing-stock, and I hated myself for it.

Even my balloon seemed to have grown more distant from me over the past few weeks;

now it hovered so high in the sky that it appeared as a small, golden dot. And this made me angry. Ai wouldn't have distanced himself from me when I fell into these pits of self-loathing and despair; he would have held on tighter and offered me grounding. But Ai was gone, and I had to remember that.

"Rose, you are lovely, you know? Once you get your braces removed, you'll start to feel different about yourself, I promise. I wish you could see yourself the way that I see you," Filipa said one day as she watched me slump down in my seat on the bus.

"But it's not just how *I* see myself, is it?" I grumbled. "*They* all tease me for so many different reasons, so I think you are just being biased."

"They tease you because they get a reaction from you ... and because they're idiots," Filipa said with a sad smile. "Honestly, you need to go home tonight and look in the mirror. I want you to *really* look. Look at *you*. And start to see what you *do* like, rather than focusing on what you don't. And then, I want you to ask yourself what you can change, and what you can't. And if you *can't* change it, how are you going to start to accept it? Because you have to in order to be happy. How are you going to accept that part which you don't like but which helps to make the lovely you, *you*?"

I glowered at my beautiful friend, and swallowed the bitter words that were threatening to spill out of my mouth. Of course it was easy for her to say that! I bet when *she* looked in the mirror, all she saw *were* parts that she liked.

But Filipa's expression was only full of love and acceptance for me. She was being genuine, and that made her even more beautiful in my eyes. So, I relaxed my scowl and nodded.

"I'll try," I mumbled.

"Good! And I want to see a list tomorrow!" my friend replied.

爱

Later that night, after the dinner dishes had been washed and put away, I excused myself from our family television time and crept upstairs to the bathroom. Shutting the door behind me, I walked over to the bathroom mirror where it hung on the wall above the sink.

Taking a deep breath, I switched on the little bar light and leaned forward to look at my reflection.

Tears welled up in an instant, and I bent

The Origami Balloon

my head, leaning on the sink. Why was this so hard? I gave myself a good talking to and tried again.

This time, I forced myself to keep looking. As tears wetted my cheeks, I cringed as I saw how angry and bumpy my facial skin looked. It didn't seem fair that someone who washed their face twice daily with natural soaps would end up with skin like this. But, that wasn't the point of the exercise. I had to look and see what I liked, what I didn't, what I could change and what I couldn't. I had to be objective.

So, it was clear that I didn't like my skin. Could I change it? Probably not, as I had tried many different lotions over the last couple of years to help with the acne, and nothing had worked. But, maybe I could buy some of that make-up that I'd seen the other girls wear. Nothing too over-the-top; just enough to take the redness away. This thought cheered me instantly. And surely the acne would go away once puberty was over and the hormones had settled down?

Next ... my glasses. And my eyes. It felt strange looking so intensely into my own eyes, but I got rather a shock. I had found something that I quite liked. My eyes were quite pretty, and I'd never noticed before that they had little hazel flecks in the deep brown of the irises.

I liked the shape of my eyes too, even though I'd been teased about that before in the past, and my lashes were long and silky. In that moment, I realized that I had let other people's prejudices impede on my own self-reflection. I had pretty eyes! And my new glasses framed them nicely—not too big and not too heavy.

I hated my mouth, but true to the experiment that I was conducting, I was able to rationalize that I actually hated my braces. This was good! The metal monstrosities would soon come off, so I tried to focus on my teeth behind the braces. They were small and white; quite inoffensive really. Filipa was right. Once my braces were removed, my mouth would no longer offer the bullies any fodder.

Like my lashes, my hair was long and silky. I had always appreciated my hair—mainly as a curtain—but, nonetheless, I had no issue with my hair.

My body then. My skinny, straight-up-and-down body. I sighed. I ate like a horse, so there was no hope of me putting on weight that way. *Nothing* was going to change my body shape, except maybe some cosmetic surgery like the kind that I'd heard some celebrities were starting to get. A bit drastic for me! Nope. I *had* hoped that puberty would have been kind to me, but … Here was something that I had to try and accept. If I could.

Feeling quite proud of myself, I brushed my teeth and washed my face before flicking off the little light. It was still quite early, but I fancied curling up in bed with the latest book that I'd borrowed from the library. I'd nearly finished it, and I wanted to discover how it ended. It was full of Chinese myth and legend, and I had enjoyed exploring the oriental world between its pages.

As I tucked myself up, cozy under the blankets, I gazed out towards the green ash tree; its canopy was glowing golden in the twilight. Next to it, also golden and back to resuming its normal position was my balloon, bobbing gently up and down.

"Decided to come closer again, did you?" I huffed, tutting as I turned my back to it and opened my book at the marker.

爱

The next day, I took the bus to City Library once school was finished. I loved this building, as it was the gateway to thousands of lifetimes and millions of realms. Although fairly new, the architect had put a lot of thought into creating this masterpiece, from the bright red brickwork to the enormous carved stone owls which perched atop.

As I entered the huge, glass atrium, I felt all of my stresses and pressures release from my body. I felt safe in here. Over the years, books had become friends to me, and they also provided me with much-needed escapism.

I walked between the stacks, trailing my fingertips along the spines of the paperbacks, waiting for one to jump out at me. I had read lots of these already, but there were still so many more to discover. I liked to shut my eyes and let the books lead me to the one I would choose; it was like a little game. And it had not let me down yet!

"*Oomph!*"

My eyes snapped open as I collided with someone. I hadn't seen anyone else between the stacks, so this was unexpected. My fingertips still lingered on the spine of a book; a book that was being tilted off the shelf by a boy who was similar in age to me.

"Oh! I am so sorry!" I said as my cheeks blazed.

"Ha, don't worry about it," said the boy with an easy smile. "I see that you were employing the good old 'fingertips leading the way' tactic!"

"You know about that?" I said as I smiled, covering my mouth with my hand.

"Of course! I believe that books speak to us, if you close your eyes and listen! My name's Matthew, by the way."

Realizing that I was just staring at him, no doubt with a ridiculous expression on my face, I dipped my head to hide behind my hair. Matthew was saying words that I really resonated with. Up until now, I had never met anyone who had felt about books as I did or who had sensed the magic they offered.

"Rose," I mumbled.

"Pardon me?"

"My name ... is Rose."

I dared to look up, and Matthew was staring at me.

"So, Rose," he said, "which has been your favorite book so far, and why?"

And just like that, I'd found my first crush. We lost three hours in the library that day, discussing our favorite stories and the authors who had inspired us the most. Matthew was easy to talk to, and he asked lots of questions, but not in a way that made me uncomfortable. He wanted to know all about my Chinese heritage, and at one point we found a book on Mahjong so that I could provide visuals to my explanations of this family game. He was fascinated.

"In some ways, it sounds a bit like the game I play with my family called Gin Rummy," he said. "Have you heard of it?"

When I confessed that I had not, Matthew made it his mission to teach me. The next Friday, he met me in the library armed with a deck of cards. He had the patience of a saint, but I had to admit that I was as awful at playing this game as I was with Mahjong.

Soon, it became a long-standing arrangement between the two of us to meet every Friday in the library. Organically, we established a kind of mini book club where we would share our thoughts about the book we had just finished, and, depending on the feedback, the other person would either borrow it themselves, or place it back on the stack. I really began to look forward to these afternoons.

And so, I think, did Matthew.

Becoming Mei-Rose

自爱
Angel Island

At the beginning of the summer break before my sophomore year, my hideous braces finally came off to reveal small, white, straight teeth. They looked reassuringly normal, and I breathed a sigh of relief. My whole mouth felt lighter somehow.

That Friday, I waited for Matthew in our usual spot in the library. It was the last time we'd meet before I went off on vacation with my family again. This time we were heading to San Francisco, and I was excited to see the Golden Gate Bridge. I was also looking forward to visiting Angel Island, where many Chinese immigrants had been processed as they entered America between 1910 and 1940. This was a part of my Chinese American history that I wanted to understand more about.

Wing, on the other hand, was more excited about our booked trip to Alcatraz. The thought of that actually terrified me, even though I knew the infamous inhabitants were long gone.

I jumped as I felt a tap on my shoulder.

"Hey! Sorry! I thought you'd heard me call to you," said Matthew as he laughed at my reaction.

"Oh! No, I didn't," I said, grinning at him. "I was lost in my thoughts, thinking about my vacation!"

"Well … look at you, all braces-less! How does it feel?"

"It feels great!" I said, automatically covering my mouth out of habit. "I don't have to worry about the bullies anymore. Well, at least about my teeth."

Matthew leaned over and gently lowered my arm.

"Stop hiding your smile, Rose. I've never liked how you do that. The bullies are lowlifes, so don't give them the satisfaction!"

I blushed and bowed my head, feeling the normal flush beginning to prickle my skin.

"So," I said, trying to dissolve my awkwardness, "what did you think of The Handmaid's Tale?"

"Oh, my goodness!" said Matthew. "Well, it—"

And so we slipped into our comfortable world of books and other realms as I watched my friend become quite animated about this latest read. I couldn't help but smile, and this time I left my hand on my lap.

爱

Two days later, we were all packed and ready to go. This was going to be a long road trip, so we were planning stopovers for two nights: the first in Omaha, and the second in Salt Lake City. Ju and I would be sharing a room, like we had each year since our trip to Washington.

I spent much of the first day's travel with my nose stuck in The Handmaid's Tale, while Wing and Ling played Chinese Checkers and Chinese Chess until Wing accused Ling of cheating.

At last we reached our motel for the night, and we were all eager to stretch our legs and find our rooms. Nǎinai and Yéyé had the usual packed feast waiting for us, and the aromas that permeated the room as they unlocked the lids of the containers make my stomach rumble. Soon we were devouring steamed vermicelli buns, chow mein, braised pork balls in gravy and Peking roasted duck.

Once we had cleared our plates, Yéyé, Uncle Bao and Bàba began discussing the latest movements in the stock market, and Auntie Lian and Māmā began to gossip about news they had heard from people at the market. Wing had his head stuck in a paleontologist manual, and Ling was reading a comic. So, Ju and I excused ourselves and disappeared to our room.

As soon as the door closed, we jumped onto our twin beds and sat facing each other, legs crossed. "So," I said, "tell me this great secret of yours!"

"Well," Ju giggled. "I've got a boyfriend!"

"What?" I squealed before clamping my hand over my mouth as I remembered that the adults were next door.

"*Shh!*" Ju whispered crossly. "You don't know how thin these walls are!"

I scooted over to the edge of the bed, eager to hear more. "Tell me everything," I whispered back. "Have you kissed?"

Ju nodded her head and grinned at me. "Don't look so shocked!" she said. "I *am* nearly 18! I'll be off to college next year."

"Do Uncle Bao and Auntie Lian know?"

"Of course not! You know as well as I do that there should be no dating, but Mei ... it's not like my friends don't have boyfriends! Everyone does. Well, nearly everyone. And Mike is so cute!"

"Mike? Is he even Chinese?"

"*Aiii-ya*! You sound like my mother, Mei! No, he is not Chinese, but it's not as if I'm telling you that I'm marrying him. Although ..." and then she threw a pillow at me, laughing loudly.

A bang on the wall let us know that we needed to quieten down, so we spent the next few minutes getting ourselves ready for bed. All this time, I mulled over my cousin's shocking disclosure. Uncle Bao and Auntie Lian would be furious with Ju if they found out, and I was astonished that my cousin would take such a risk. But then, part of me was also impressed that she was confident enough to be *more American*, as my mother would say.

Māmā was forever bemoaning the teenage sitcoms that aired on the television. She let everyone know that she thought there was *far* too much hanky-panky going on and not enough studying. Her repetitive mantra seemed to be, "It's not our way, Mei. They have their ways and we have ours. So please don't try to be more American." It was so confusing, and here was my very own cousin, my *Chinese* cousin no less, doing exactly that. I felt a little thrill of excitement.

As we snuggled under our blankets, I couldn't help myself as I asked, "What is it like?"

"*Hmmm*? What's what like?"

"Kissing."

"*Oooooh*," said Ju, rolling over onto her side to face me with her eyes bright. "Well, at first I didn't like it because it was a bit wet and we kept bumping teeth. Also, we made funny noises, which was a bit embarrassing. But then, with some practice we got better at it, and now it's nice."

"Nice, how?"

"Well, you're getting close to someone you have a crush on and who has a crush on you. You kind of get used to how they kiss and then your lips just ... match. It gives you a sort of tingly feeling."

Ju then rolled onto her stomach and rested her head on her hand as she peered at me. "Why do you want to know, anyway? Is there someone *you'd* like to kiss? What about that Matthew you've been telling me about, *hmmm*?"

"No," I squeaked as I pulled my blanket up over my head, which just made Ju laugh all the more. I took a breath and peeked out at her again. "I just wanted to know ... for whenever!"

"*Ahh*, I see," she smiled at me. "But tell me more about Matthew. He seems nice."

"He is, but we're just friends. Why are you looking at me like that? We are!" I insisted. "He's your age and I bet he just sees me as a little sister type of thing. We just both love books. That's all. Honestly!"

"If you say so," said Ju as she settled back down again. "We'll see!"

爱

It was incredible to see the Golden Gate Bridge as it crested the horizon in front of us. We had specifically taken the road to the city that would lead us over this incredible suspension bridge, and it did not disappoint. Even Wing put down his dinosaur book to marvel at the engineering ingenuity of its design. We had also timed our arrival to perfection as we crossed the bridge at sunset; it was picture postcard perfect.

Once we had unpacked, we found San Francisco's Chinatown to dine out for the evening. There was no depriving Yéyé of his rice after all! Halfway through our first course, Uncle Bao turned to Ju.

"Gūniáng, do you remember Wang Chaoxiang and his family? He has a son just a few years older than you, called Wang Huan, I believe."

Ju choked on her chow mein as she looked up at her father. "*Ermm* ... I vaguely remember

Huan, Bàba. He used to kick my leg when we sat in church!"

"Oh Ju," laughed Auntie Lian. "You do remember the funniest of things!"

"Well, he has turned into a very respectable young man ... training to become a surgeon now. I am told that he has just the sort of character traits that you would look for in a husband. Just so you know, your mother and I have invited the Wang family over for dinner when we return from our vacation."

I gaped at Ju as she continued to stare at her parents. She looked horrified.

"Close your mouth, gūniáng," said Uncle Bao. "You are not a goldfish."

Mine and Ju's mouths snapped shut at the same time, and my cousin stole a glance my way. All I could do was shrug and offer her a hopeful smile. We would be talking about this later on once we got back to our room, but for now, all we could do was enjoy our dinner of stir-fried tofu and rice.

"Maybe you'll find that you like him," I said to a sulky Ju later that evening, once we had been allowed to return to our room.

"I don't *want* to like him. The thought of my own parents trying to pick my husband for me is just ... plain weird!"

"At least arranged marriages have been banned, so they can't force you to marry him," I said with a chuckle, trying to lighten the mood, but all I got in reply was a glare. So I tried a different approach. "Well, maybe they're just hoping that you'll like him because they know you'll have a secure future with him."

"Mei! I'm still young! I don't want to think about getting married, for goodness' sake! I want to go to college and have some fun before I settle down!"

"*Aiii-ya*! What *kind* of fun? Fun with Mike, you mean?"

Ju waggled her eyebrows at me and burst out laughing as my face gave away my shock once more. "God, no!" she then said, sobering up immediately as she realized what I was thinking. "I'm not talking about *that* kind of fun. No, I may not be following *all* of the rules, but I would never break *that* one! My husband will be my one and only, but not for a long time yet!"

"Well, okay then! So, what are you going to do about Huan?"

"What can I do? I would never dream of bringing dishonor on our family, so I'll just have to see what happens when it happens, I suppose." Ju sighed and then rolled onto her back. "Night, night, Mei."

"Night. And try not to worry about it or let it spoil your vacation. It'll all work out as it's meant to in the end."

爱

The next day, it was time for our trip to Alcatraz. To say that I was nervous was a massive understatement. Nobody really understood my anxiety though, so I tried to keep it to myself.

We boarded the ferry that would take us to the abandoned federal prison, and Wing started taking pictures of everything that moved, including many of the gulls that circled the boat. The water was quite choppy, which didn't help my already nervous disposition, so I sat down on my seat and closed my eyes. I felt a tug at my chest, and I put this down to my nerves, but when it came again, I opened my eyes ... and smiled.

I hadn't seen my origami balloon since leaving home, but here it was now, bobbing along beside me. Just when I needed it. A sense of calm passed through me, and I let out a long, steady breath as I closed my eyes again and tilted my face to the breeze from the bay.

The ferry ride was over soon enough, and

when I opened my eyes again, the balloon had gone. Where to? I had no idea, but my sense of calm remained.

The exterior of Alcatraz was exactly as I had imagined it would be: imposing, unwelcoming, sterile. A shiver ran down my spine as Wing went off clicking his camera and jabbering on about facts he had learned about this place to anyone who would listen. But only one word came to my mind when thinking about this island: eerie.

We were taken on a tour by a guide who was as animated as my brother, and we were regaled with information about previous convicts and their shackled arrivals—which apparently had been a source of great interest for the island's younger inhabitants back in the day.

I hadn't realized until then that the prison staff and their families had lived on the island in the old military installation, taking a boat to the mainland once a week for groceries. I felt another shiver go down my spine as I contemplated life growing up in this dismal setting. But the guide assured us that life had been quite fun for the children as they fished in the bay and had well-stocked games rooms to enjoy.

Once inside the main building of the prison, Ling took my hand as we walked the hallways, surrounded by metal bars and concrete cells.

"You okay, mèimei?" I said, and she bobbed her head whilst looking around wide-eyed.

"Oh, jiějiě," she whispered. "Do you feel like we are being watched?"

"Yes, I feel it too … maybe it's the ghosts of the convicts, forever trapped within these walls?"

"Oh! Don't say that! That's terrifying!"

I squeezed her hand and closed my eyes, tuning out the voice of the guide, who was now recounting the occasion when Al Capone had spent time in the facility and informing his audience where the gangster's cell had been. Ling let go of my hand, no doubt to follow the others, while I remained there, eyes shut and my imagination working up a storm.

I believed that I could hear metal cups being banged against metal bars and lots of shouting out. I heard the guards blowing their whistles to restore peace. I heard sobbing. Lots of sobbing. It was heartbreaking.

Opening my eyes, I took one more look around this place, whose very walls seemed to be saturated with fear, anger and sadness, and then I left to wait for my family outside.

爱

The rest of the vacation flew by with lots of barbeques and family games in the parks. We made all of the quintessential tourist trips to various museums and art galleries, but the one I was most keen to visit didn't come until the end of our two-week jaunt.

Angel Island.

We caught the 9:45 a.m. ferry across to the island and decided to make the 20-minute walk to the immigration station rather than take the tram because it was a beautiful day.

A lot of the original buildings had been destroyed in a fire in 1940. However, a deep respect shown for this period of our history meant that educational monuments had been erected in their place to share the experience of the hundreds of thousands of people who had spent time on the island before being allowed onto the mainland.

As I wandered around, I could see Chinese characters etched into the stone; poems of anguish and despair written by the immigrants, some of whom were made to stay on this island for years. The writings had been translated for everyone to read, and the tales they told meant that I soon had silent tears running down my cheeks. These people, some of them possibly from the provinces in China where Năinai and Yéyé had grown up, had come to America seeking a better life, but these poems told a very different story.

And as the thought of my grandparents passed through my mind, I glanced over to see them standing, somber, next to the monuments as they read the inscriptions of their countrymen. Maybe some neighbors that they *had* known from Fujian and Guangdong had passed through here, but that was a question too painful to ask. Năinai and Yéyé had been lucky, it would seem, emigrating just a few years after this immigration station had closed.

I wiped my eyes with the edge of my sleeve and walked over to where they were standing. Putting one of my hands into each of theirs, I gave them a squeeze. No words were needed as we stood there upon the very ground where so many Chinese people had met America for the very first time, and we bowed our heads in deference. I wished that it could have been a warmer welcome for them all those years earlier.

"Lái," said Māmā, breaking the silence. "A guide has just told me of a perfect picnic spot.

Becoming Mei-Rose

Hurry, as we have a climb ahead of us!"

And so we began our hour-long ascent of Mount Livermore, finding the most beautiful vista at the top: a 360-degree view of San Francisco Bay. While Wing grabbed his camera once more, Ju, Ling and I helped Māmā and Auntie Lian to lay out the picnic blankets and prepare the food.

We spent an incredibly relaxing couple of hours contemplating all that we had learned on our trip, and as I gazed out upon the beauty of the bay, I was aware of my imaginary balloon bobbing softly behind me, just a fingertip out of reach.

自爱

Chinese New Year

My sophomore year was fairly uneventful. On the whole, the bullies left me alone. Possibly it was due to Filipa's "mama bear" presence; possibly it was due to the fact that I showed no reaction anymore to the taunts. But whatever it was, I was given my first few months of peace since starting school all those years before. That is, until the week before the Christmas holidays when Kendal and her cronies cornered me in the restroom by the science block.

Filipa was off sick that day, so I had walked to my next class on my own, stopping off at the restroom on the way.

"Oh lookie, lookie here!" said a taunting voice as I washed my hands, and I looked into the mirror to see Kendal, Sophie, Katie and another two girls who I didn't know crowd around behind me. "Where's your Spanish pit-bull today? Have you taken her back to the pound?"

All the girls laughed as I looked back

down at my soapy hands.

"She's Portuguese actually, Kendal," I said, my voice surprisingly steady despite the anxiety beginning to well up in the pit of my stomach. "Get your geography right."

Someone grabbed a handful of my hair and tugged it hard, pulling my head back so that my neck jarred painfully.

"Portuguese, Spanish, *Chinese* ... what do I care?" said Kendal as she glared down at me, her hand tightening in my hair. "You're all mongrels to me! You're not American, are you? You don't belong here! *Look* at you, for goodness sake! With your ugly eyes and stupid clothes! You're pathetic!" Then she gave my head a shove as she let it go, and I just caught my balance against the sink before I went headfirst into the wall.

Fighting the tears which were threatening to fall, I took a deep breath, rested both hands on the sink and raised my chin up high as I looked at my nemesis once more in the mirror.

"I *am* American, actually. I was born here, just like you. And my eyes are pretty to me, so that's all that matters. *You're* the ugly one, Kendal. Maybe not on the outside, but definitely on the inside with all of your horrible thoughts and mean words. What have I ever done to you? I don't deserve this hate from you ... I'm a good person. But you don't see that because I look different to you. And, so what? You think that I look different so I must be all wrong, and to be all right I need to look like you? I don't think so! I'm happy being me any day of the week."

And with that, I turned around to face Kendal properly, my jaw set. These were the most words that I had ever uttered in one go in my life, but there was a fire in my chest that I felt proud of. Until the hand slapped me hard across my face, making my glasses tumble with a clatter to the tiled floor.

I heard it before I felt it, but then my cheek began to sting as my own hand rose to cover it. This time I couldn't stop the tears as they fell to mark my humiliation.

"Don't you *ever* try to say that you are better than me!" Kendal hissed close to my face, and then she laughed as I shrank back. "Yes, you better believe it! Cower away! Speak to me like that again, and I'll put you on the floor. Got it? C'mon girls, let's get away from this mutt before we all get fleas!"

As the restroom door banged against the wall, I slid down the wall to sit on the tiled floor. I reached out and retrieved my glasses as my bullies' laughter faded when the door closed behind them. Bringing my knees up to my chest, I rested my forehead on them and sobbed my heart out. Why hadn't Kendal understood that I was trying to say that I was just different, not better? Why was it so important for everyone to look a certain way in order to be accepted? Yes, I was Chinese. But I was also American, so I had the right to be here as much as Kendal had!

Now, I just felt angry, and I lifted my head from my knees, taking off my glasses to wipe my eyes with my hand. When I put my glasses back on, I was startled to see my balloon bobbing up and down right in front of my face.

I stared at it for a couple of moments before it edged nearer and bopped me gently on the head. I laughed and scrambled to my feet just as the restroom door swung open again and some juniors came in, chatting away. They stopped as they looked at me, taking in my watery eyes and red cheek.

"You okay?" one of them asked.

"Yes! Yes I am now, thank you!" I said as I smiled at them, and then I walked out of the restroom, my head held high, and down the hallway to my next class.

"Oh wow! You go, girl!" laughed Filipa the next day when I told her what had happened. "It looks like some of my fire has rubbed off on you! I'm super proud of you for standing up to her like that!"

"Didn't stop her from slapping me though," I grumbled.

"Oh, don't you worry! She'll get what's coming to her," said Filipa, and I looked at her whilst raising my eyebrows. "Don't worry! *I'm* not going to do anything ... you handled yourself brilliantly! No ... I'm talking about karma. You know? What goes around comes around? Just sit back, my friend, and watch the universe play its hand!"

We both laughed then and stepped off the bus to begin another day at school.

爱

I still loved my Saturday job at *Bunty's Cookies and Cakes*. Auntie Bunty had such a lovely, kind heart, and she spent so much time teaching me how to make the most perfect pastries, cookies and muffins, all of which melted in the mouth.

As Chinese New Year approached, I decided to broach something that I had been thinking about for a while, and I trusted Auntie Bunty enough to run it by her.

"Auntie Bunty?"

"Yes, my dear," said my boss as she finished cashing up the register for the afternoon. The café's last customer had been gently ushered out of the door, and I was now preparing to wipe down all of the tables.

"I was wondering if you would allow me to try something."

"What did you have in mind, Rose?"

"Well, you know how I always struggle to work out how my Chinese and American parts go together?"

"Uhh hmm."

"Do you think that I could use your bakery to experiment with cakes for Chinese New Year? I thought it could be fun if we offer Chinese cake options alongside American ones and see how they are received by the customers?"

"Well now, what an interesting thought! Yes … I like it, Rose! It could be a nice twist to offer customers new produce whilst celebrating the diversity in our city. How clever!"

I blushed at Auntie Bunty's compliment and clapped my hands in glee. "Great," I said, "I'll start looking up recipes straight away."

So later, as soon as my chores at home

were completed, I pulled all of Māmā's recipe books down from her shelf in the kitchen and began my research. Ling came in to find me scribbling notes from the open tomes spread across the kitchen table.

"What are you up to, jiějiě?" she said.

"Auntie Bunty has given me the go-ahead to create some Chinese cakes and desserts to sell in the café for Chinese New Year!"

I was so excited with this project that it must have been evident on my face, and Ling stood there grinning back at me.

"Do you want some help?"

I nodded as I patted the bench beside me, and I pushed the notepad and pencil her way as I pulled one huge recipe book towards me.

"You can make the notes and help me to decide which ones to choose," I said.

Two hours later, we had our list of sweet delicacies that I would suggest to Auntie Bunty next Saturday when I went to work, and we decided that before then we would practice making some of them at home. With Ling agreeing to be my commis chef, we were keen to start the next day. Māmā agreed to give us free rein in the kitchen based on our promise to sell what we made in order to reimburse her for the ingredients used.

So, the next morning, Ling and I set to work. First of all we tackled the jian dui (sesame balls). I had always loved the chewy but crunchy texture of these treats, and their nutty taste was sublime.

I heated the oil in our wok while Ling spread some sesame seeds out on some parchment paper, and then she dissolved some brown sugar in the water that was boiling in another pan. Once she had finished, I poured the rice flour into a large bowl and added the dissolved sugar solution, mixing it all together until I had a nice, sticky dough.

Then came the fun part. Ling and I each took a small piece of dough, about the size of a golf ball, and pressed each of them into small bowl shapes. We then added a teaspoon of sweet red bean paste into the dents that we had created, and we closed the dough over the top, ensuring that the bean paste was completely sealed. Each of our balls was then dipped in cool water and rolled over the sesame seeds.

We worked really well together, and soon we had a decent pile of equally-sized sesame balls waiting to be fried. Making sure that we had our aprons on, Ling began to pass me ball after ball, which I lowered into the hot oil. We had to do batches so that the balls didn't stick together in the wok. By the time the jian dui were cooked, they had grown to be three times their original size.

We popped the balls onto paper towels to drain the excess oil, and then we placed five of them on a separate plate for Bàba, Māmā, Wing, Ling and I to try. Next, we collected the cardboard sign that we had made earlier and the glass jar for the coins that we would earn, and we went out onto the street to sell the remaining jian dui that we had placed in our large bamboo bowl.

Soon enough, all of the jian dui had gone, and the compliments from our customers reassured us that our efforts had not been in vain.

Next, we wanted to try the nian gao, or Chinese New Year cake. Māmā had once told me that sticky rice symbolized prosperity, and so too did this cake.

Once the cane sugar and brown sugar had melted in the water, I mixed sesame seed paste with coconut milk and then added this to the melted sugar. Then we popped this in with wheat starch and rice flour and mixed it well. Ling added the pinch of salt to finish it off. It took us ages to remove all of the lumps from the batter, but soon it was smooth and we could add the vegetable oil before mixing it again well.

Once we had poured the batter into a cake pan, we set the pressure cooker to the right temperature and steamed our nian gao. After the allotted time for steaming, I skewered the cake with a chopstick, and we were delighted to see the end of the chopstick reappear with nothing stuck to it. Our cake was done. Ling stuck a red date on top to cover the hole I had made, and then we popped the cake into the fridge for a few hours to cool.

That evening, Ling and I proudly served the nian gao for dessert after pan-frying it in eggs, which gave it a crispy outer texture whilst the inside remained lovely and chewy.

"Well done, gūniáng," Bàba said as he wiped his mouth with his napkin. "Very sweet and tasty!"

High praise indeed from our father! Ling and I grinned at each other, and we tucked into our own slices.

Over the course of the week, we practiced making Hong Kong egg tarts, which looked a bit like the western custard tarts that we made in the bakery. The traditional Chinese pastry bases were tricky to make though, so I decided that I would ask Auntie Bunty to help me to make our usual puff pastry ones instead because they would be easier to produce for our customers.

We also created buttery Chinese almond cookies, which symbolized the coins given at New Year to represent good fortune. Chinese doughnut sticks, or youtiao, were a staple food in our house, so I didn't feel like I needed practice with these, but we did make the pillowy pineapple buns and ma lai go (Chinese steamed cake), which originated in Malaysia but which had been adopted by the Cantonese.

The ma lai go I found tricky because I had to keep throwing away my starter dough, but I got there in the end. Our final cake was fluffy and gooey at the same time, and it was absolutely delicious.

Next, we enjoyed making the Chinese five spice chocolate pots de crème. These were like a chocolaty custard made from cream, fine chocolate, egg yolk and milk, and they were seasoned with anise, cloves, cinnamon, fennel and pepper. I envisioned serving these in Auntie Bunty's floral teacups with a teaspoon on the saucer for their consumption.

Then, we made the sachima. This was always on our table on Chinese New Year, so this was why Ling and I had chosen it. Made from fried flour dough strips, which I placed in a baking tin, covered with syrup and sesame seeds and compressed before baking, these looked a little like the western Rice Krispie cakes when they were served.

Finally, to the Chinese New Year menu I decided to also add Chinese milk tea, which was black tea and milk with white tapioca pearls added to it—these made it bubbly!

Our neighbors enjoyed a veritable feast by the time Ling and I had finished practicing, and we earned enough money to pay back Māmā for her ingredients, and then some. I was so excited to go to work on Saturday to share with Auntie Bunty what we had done.

My boss and mentor could not have been prouder. She insisted that I showed her how to make everything so, after the café had closed, we spent several fun hours as I taught her how to make these authentic Chinese desserts. The student had become the teacher, and I realized how much I enjoyed creating these edible pieces of heaven for others.

Chinese New Year was the following Saturday, so by the time I left to go home that evening, we both had a clear understanding of how we wanted the day to go. Auntie Bunty was going to decorate the café with Chinese lanterns, and she was planning on removing the gingham tablecloths and replacing the vases of pretty flowers with red and gold candles.

Becoming Mei-Rose

It was going to be the year of the snake, so we agreed that Ling and I would create a large banner depicting a beautiful snake with golden, red and green scales, which we would hang behind the counter. I was so excited, and I loved that Auntie Bunty had embraced this aspect of my heritage so willingly and fully.

When the day came, I arrived at the bakery at 6:30 a.m. Auntie Bunty had just arrived, and together we powered up the ovens and hobs and began our mammoth task of creating both the Chinese delicacies and the American ones. By the time 9 a.m. arrived, we were both slightly frazzled but invigorated for the day ahead.

It could not have been a greater success. Our regulars raved about the Chinese options, and many asked where I had learned to create such beautiful desserts. When I explained that they could find many of these in Chinatown on the dim sum carts or in the restaurants, they were amazed.

"Would we be allowed to visit there?" they asked.

"Of course!" I said. "The more the merrier!"

And when 5 p.m. came, Auntie Bunty and I collapsed onto the nearest chairs and congratulated the success of the day over Chinese milk tea and the last of the jian dui.

"This is your calling, Rose," Auntie Bunty said. "This is what you need to be doing … bringing this wonderful part of your heritage into the western streets of America. It's all well and good that people can find these dishes in Chinatown, but many won't venture there for one reason or another. But, can you imagine *you* with your own café offering oriental catering on these very streets? They demolished the lot today! You should be very proud. You have done well, my dear. Very well."

I grinned at Auntie Bunty. "Thank you for giving me the opportunity."

"You have become like a grandchild to me, Rose," said Auntie Bunty fondly. "I have no family of my own, but I hope you don't mind me saying that I have grown very attached to you over the years."

I swallowed my tears as I got up and gave my boss the biggest hug I could muster. "Thank you," I mumbled, unable to say anymore due to the emotion that I was feeling.

It was now the summer semester, and Matthew

and I were sitting in our usual little nook in the library, dissecting our favorite, and not-so-favorite, books.

"So," said Matthew, looking a little embarrassed and unwilling to meet my gaze. "My prom is obviously happening this year …"

I looked up as he spoke, unsure as to what he was implying.

"Oh, of course," I said. "Ju's is this year too! She's taking her fiancé, Huan."

I laughed as I recalled the conversation that I'd had with Ju all those months before when she had been adamant that she was far too young for marriage. As it turned out, as soon as she had clapped eyes on Wang Huan, she had been smitten, and he with her. I hadn't seen her since the news of their engagement had been announced, but we were due for our annual vacation soon where we would catch up on all of our news and celebrate her betrothal.

"Oh … really … right … *ermm*," Matthew said as I looked at him, concerned.

"Are you okay?"

"Yes … I … *ermm* … was wondering if you would like to come with me … to mine?"

"What? No!" I almost shrieked, and Matthew looked mortified. "I mean," I said, "Why would you want *me* to go?"

Matthew stared at me, and I couldn't understand why I could see hurt in his eyes. "Oh, don't worry," he said eventually. "It was just an idea."

"Oh right," I laughed. "Thank goodness! Can you imagine?"

Matthew stood up abruptly. "I need to go now, Rose. I'll see you later."

"What? Why—"

But he was gone. And the ache in my chest was unbearable as I watched him walk away. I couldn't run after him to ask him what was wrong; I wouldn't, as I'd probably only trip over something and make a complete fool of myself. But as I watched him disappear from sight, I knew that somehow I had made a huge mistake.

I left the library feeling like a hollow shell. And to make matters worse, my balloon appeared. Only now, it was hovering high above me as if scolding me for my behavior.

"I don't understand," I called out to it, making several people around me jump and quickly move away from me. "What did I do?"

But the balloon just bobbed up and down at a distance, making me feel so alone once again.

自爱

A Bonding and Breaking of Hearts

I lost count of the number of Fridays that I waited in the little library nook for Matthew to come. But he never did. It was clear that our little book club had now been reduced to a lonely, solitary member, but I still couldn't fathom out what I had done wrong. I was half-tempted to take a bus to his school and wait for him outside, but I wasn't sure that he would want to see me if he was so resolute in avoiding the library.

During the last week of the semester, Filipa innocently brought him up in conversation because she was unaware of what had happened, and I had been too embarrassed to tell her about it.

"Will you be seeing Matthew over the summer break this year?" she asked.

"*Errmm* … no. No, I won't," I muttered, as I started plucking at the hem of my skirt. Out of the corner of my eye, I could see Filipa studying me, so I chose to stare out of the bus window instead.

"Out with it! What's going on, Rose? I can always tell when you're trying to hide something from me."

"*Aii-ya*! I'm not trying to hide anything. It's just … well, I think … no, I know … that I've upset him somehow, and now he's avoiding me," I said miserably.

"Since when?" said Filipa.

"Since a few weeks ago. Like, since the beginning of the semester …"

"Oh! You never said! What on earth did you do? You and he were such great friends!"

"Yes … well, apparently not," I mumbled. "And I have no idea what I did, honestly! He just started joking around, out of the blue, saying that I should go to his prom with him. But then he got all funny with me when I laughed it off, and then he walked away. That's the last time I saw him."

"Oh, *Rose*," groaned Filipa, staring at me as if I was dense. "You honestly don't know how you offended him?"

"No! And there's no point in you looking at me like that. If I knew how to fix it, I would have done so by now!"

"I don't know whether to laugh or cry! You are such a nincompoop! It's so obvious why

Matthew is avoiding you!"

"Is it?" I snapped at my friend. "Well, please enlighten me!"

"*Was* he joking around about you going to the prom with him? Think back carefully. How *exactly* did he say it?"

"Of course he was joking!"

"No. Think properly!"

"Well ... he was kind of embarrassed, I suppose," I said, frowning, "and he just sort of blurted it out."

"And you said?"

"No, of course! I wouldn't have wanted to embarrass him, for goodness' sake. I'm like a little sister to him!"

"Are you? Says who? Did Matthew say that?"

"Well, no, but, come on ..."

"Come on, what? Shall I tell you what's happened here? And hear me out! Because I am so fed up of you not seeing what other people see, Rose Lee!"

I gawked at my friend as she turned to face me directly, and it was fair to say that she looked a little agitated.

"You," she said, "need to start realizing what a gift you are to others. I bet that Matthew has *never* seen you as a little sister. He was asking you to his prom because he liked you. As in, *liked* you, liked you ... and you turned him down. Well, laughed in his face, by the sounds of it!"

My mouth dropped open as I considered what Filipa was saying. "No," I said. "It wasn't like that!"

"Wasn't it? Let me get this right. These are the facts *you* just told me. Firstly, he looked embarrassed when he was asking you. Secondly, he blurted out his invitation. And thirdly, he walked off when you told him no and laughed at him about it? Am I right?"

"Well, yes, I suppose, when you put it like that, but ..."

"No buts! Those are all hallmark traits of a boy asking out a girl who he likes and then disappearing in a hurry because he is mortified that he's been turned down. Oh Rose!"

The silence between us was deafening as Filipa's words percolated around inside my head, and I had to accept the truth of them regardless of how alien it seemed. I looked at my friend, who just shook her head in frustration.

"This is all about you not thinking you're worthy enough!" she said. "You *assumed* he was joking because you can't imagine *why* he would like you in the first place. Because you *still* can't look at yourself and see the beautiful person that

I see ... that Matthew saw!"

Filipa was sounding angry now, and I put my hand on her arm to try and comfort her. "No!" she said, shaking it off as she stood up to exit the bus at her stop. "When are you going to stop giving yourself such a hard time and start accepting that *you*, Rose Lee, deserve to be loved?"

And with that, Filipa stomped off the bus without looking back. I could feel other passengers staring at me, so I slid down in my seat and bowed my head to let my curtain of hair hide my flushed face.

As I walked from my own bus stop to home, Filipa's words kept repeating on a loop in my mind. She had been so angry with me.

This is all about you not thinking you're worthy enough! When are you going to stop giving yourself such a hard time and start accepting that you, Rose Lee, deserve to be loved?

I could see my balloon floating ahead of me as I walked. It had maintained its distance since the day that Matthew had walked away from me, and now a weird idea presented itself in my mind; a hypothesis which had formed through Filipa's words and the strange behavior of my golden companion.

Filipa was right. I *had* laughed at

Matthew's invitation because I had been terrified of the thought that he might have actually liked me in *that* way. Of course, I adored him—I had from the moment that we had met. But I had convinced myself, as Filipa had been quick to see, that it could have never amounted to anything more than a friendship. Deep down, I had known that Matthew's invitation was genuine, but I had panicked; in that moment, I had managed to convince myself that he would soon come to realize that he had made a mistake, and I had decided to save us both the embarrassment. Why? Because I did not think I was deserving of his love. There. I had said it. I had admitted it.

"Am I right?" I called up to my balloon—fortunately this time, the street was deserted. "You came so close when I stood up for myself in the restroom because I knew that I didn't deserve what Kendal was doing to me. And now you have gone so far away because I thought that Matthew was too good for me."

The origami balloon bobbed a fraction closer, as if to confirm what I had said. I felt the familiar dull ache in my chest as it did so, and it reminded me yet again of my beloved Ai. Life had been so much easier when Ai had been with me. With my arms around his neck or his head on my lap, my dog had always had a way of letting me know that I was important and valued.

I looked up at the golden balloon once more and stared at it intently. Maybe I had to do for myself what Ai used to do for me? Maybe I had to find out how to value who I was and stop relying on others to do it for me? The balloon bobbed closer.

"*Aiii-ya*! Easy for you to say!" I snapped at it as I flung myself through my front door, slamming it so hard behind me that the crockery in the kitchen rattled on the shelves.

爱

Two weeks later, Ling and I were in our room getting ready to go to Năinai's and Yéyé's because they were hosting a Chinese banquet in honor of Ju's and Huan's engagement. I couldn't wait to see my cousin; I'd missed her so much.

Ling and I were to wear matching green dresses with high necks and long sleeves. Thankfully, they had been made from light cotton, so we wouldn't swelter in the heat. When Wing came into our room, he looked very smart in his gray trousers, blue shirt and tie; he was the spitting image of Bàba.

"Stop pulling at your collar, dìdì," I

scolded. "You'll make your tie all crooked."

"*Aiii* … it's too humid! And this collar is too tight! I can barely breathe!"

"Well, you know what Māmā will say," I chuckled as Wing rolled his eyes at me.

I finished braiding Ling's hair, and then we all went downstairs to wait for our parents. I was keen to leave, as I wanted to hear every detail of the proposal from Ju. I hoped that it was the stuff of fairytales; Ju was such a hopeless romantic at heart. But then I remembered the conversation we'd had with Nǎinai and Auntie Lian years earlier, and I didn't hold out much hope.

When we arrived at Nǎinai's and Yéyé's, we could see Uncle Bao's and Auntie Lian's car parked outside, so I was quick to run up the steps and into the house to find my cousin. There she was, completely surrounded by family and friends, with Huan beaming by her side. In that moment, I didn't believe a couple could have looked any happier.

Ju saw me come in, and she gave me the biggest grin. Then she held up her left hand, wiggled her ring finger and waggled her eyebrows. Glinting on her finger was a sparkling diamond and jade ring—it was absolutely beautiful and matched the shine in her eyes.

"I got my ring," she mouthed to me across the room, and I grinned back at her, rolling my eyes in mock despair. But really, I was beyond happy for her: maybe her fairytale ending was coming true after all.

When it was time to eat, all of the guests gasped as Huan entered the room with a gift for our family—a whole roasted suckling pig.

"In our Chinese culture, roasted pork symbolizes virginity," Māmā told me, nodding her head in approval and watching as Huan placed his offering with deference in the middle of the old, rosewood table. Năinai then followed him out and added her dish of Peking duck to the feast. Finally, Auntie Lian placed lobster to the other side of the suckling pig, and Uncle Bao laughed as he saw my eyes widen in surprise—it wasn't every day that we had lobster on our table!

"Red symbolizes happiness, joy and celebration," he said, pointing to the vibrant color of the lobster's meat.

Uncle Bao then went to stand next to Auntie Lian and Ju in front of the table, opening his arms wide to invite Huan and his parents to join them too. "Wang Chaoxiang," he said as he shook his friend's hand. "I can't tell you how thrilled we are about the joining of our two families. Wang Huan has already made Ju very happy, and I foresee a positive future for them both!"

Wang Chaoxiang gripped Uncle Bao's hand firmly between his two and pumped it up and down with relish. "Lee Bao. We, too, are honored to call Ju 'gūniáng', and we look forward to the day that our families are bonded by their wedding oaths!"

Now that the parents had said their part, attention fell back on the happy couple as requests were made for them to share the auspicious date they had chosen for the actual marriage ceremony. Ju looked at her fiancé shyly, and he nodded his head as he took her hand in his and kissed the inside of her wrist.

"August 10th next year," she said as she blushed. The whole room erupted in excited chatter and many, many questions.

"And now, let's eat!" boomed Yéyé's voice, interrupting the barrage of *whats*, *whens* and *hows* that Ju and Huan were deflecting, but there was a mischievous twinkle in his eye. "This poor old man is wasting away from hunger! Now, where's the rice?"

Nǎinai tutted at her husband as everyone laughed at his joke, but then she gave him a sweet smile as she batted his hand away from the rice dish and patted his cheek. "Go, sit. I will bring you your food, old man. That way I can be sure that there will be rice left for everyone else!" And so Yéyé kissed his wife on her cheek and shuffled off to find his chair.

爱

Two nights later, just as we were getting ready for bed, the telephone rang, which was unusual for that time of night. As Bàba answered the phone and spoke rapidly in Cantonese, we froze and stood in silence staring at him, waiting to hear who it could possibly be.

"Māmā ... Māmā, màn yīdiǎn ... slow down ..." he said.

My blood ran cold, and I reached for Ling's hand as my father assured Nǎinai that he was on his way. "And Bao, Māmā? Okay ... okay."

Bàba slammed down the phone and grabbed his coat from its hook beside the front door. Turning to us he said, "Yéyé has collapsed, but I can't get more out of Nǎinai than that, so pray for him. She has phoned for an ambulance, but I need to be there when it arrives!" Turning to our mother he said, "Phone Bao. He needs to be there too."

Māmā closed the door behind Bàba and ushered us back into the living room where we sat wide-eyed and not sure of what to say or think. There was no point in trying to go to bed now, for not one of us would be able to sleep. So, we closed our eyes and began to pray silently, hoping beyond hope that our prayers would be answered. All that could be heard was the rhythmic ticking of the old ebony clock on the mantel.

As it neared midnight, the phone in the hall rang again. In the silence of night, its sound was ominous and intrusive. Māmā gestured for us to stay where we were, and she went to answer the call, closing the door behind her. I strained to hear what was being said, but only her muffled voice was audible as Ling nestled closer into me on the couch.

Wing glanced at me, obvious worry etched across his tired face, so I gave him the most reassuring smile that I could muster. Then Māmā returned, and the last remnants of hope I was clinging onto evaporated as I noted the tear tracks upon her face.

"Yéyé has gone, háizimen. He is with his angels in heaven, and he is at peace."

We all rushed to our mother and held on

to her and each other for dear life. Our beloved Yéyé! How could this be? He'd been fine at Ju's engagement party just a couple of days ago, hadn't he? It made no sense, and we couldn't begin to try and wrap our minds around it. So, we stood there, tears flowing freely, sharing in our grief as we remembered the fine man who had once crossed oceans and faced so many hardships, fighting for a better future for his family.

爱

The wake for Yéyé occurred one week later. His body had been washed and dusted with talcum powder before he was dressed in his finest black suit from his wardrobe. As per Chinese custom, all of his other clothes had been burned by Năinai, with the help of Bàba and Uncle Bao.

As Yéyé had died at home, his casket was placed on a stand in the living room, and a gong was situated to the left of the door with a white banner hanging over the entrance to the room. All of the mirrors in the house had been removed, and all of the statues of deities had been covered with red paper. Māmā had explained the reason for all of these customs, but there was so much more to learn in order for Yéyé's funeral to go without a hitch.

Wreaths, photos of Yéyé and gifts were laid at the head of the open casket, while a little altar had been erected at its feet. We lit a white candle and burned incense, and we watched as a stoic Năinai snapped Yéyé's comb in half, keeping one part for herself, and laying the second half in the coffin with her husband. His face had been covered with a yellow cloth, and his body with a blue one.

"Māmā, why are they burning prayer money?" Ling asked, watching some mourners next to the casket.

"It's to make sure that Yéyé has enough money in the afterlife," my mother replied, very matter-of-factly. "That is why we leave offerings of food for him too, look." She pointed to the edible gifts next to where Yéyé lay. "It's to make sure that he never goes hungry. And see ... there's lots of rice."

Whilst Năinai, my parents, Uncle Bao and Auntie Lian all wore black, Wing, Ling and I had been told to wear blue clothes. I was missing the company and comfort of my favorite cousin though—who would also have been wearing blue—because custom would not allow her or Huan to come to say goodbye to Yéyé.

"Engaged couples must not attend funerals as it is believed to invite misfortune into their own lives," my father had explained the day before. "Poor Huan and Ju must also show their respect by now postponing their wedding, although Uncle Bao says they will postpone it only by a year, as Nǎinai wishes for the minimum amount of disruption to their lives."

The house was full of yellow and white flowers—irises and chrysanthemums—which, together with the burning incense and prayer money, led to quite a heady scent permeating throughout the rooms. There were also many people there, paying their last respects and wailing at the loss of a dear family member and friend.

Then it came time for Yéyé to be laid to rest. His coffin was nailed shut, and we all departed the house as white and yellow holy papers were pasted to the casket. It was then carried headfirst out of the home and placed with reverence into the back of the waiting hearse.

As eldest son, Bàba was first to step forwards, closely followed by Uncle Bao, and both of them then leaned their foreheads against the hearse as it led them slowly down the road. The rest of the funeral procession came after as it made its sad way towards the cemetery.

Situated upon a hillside, the plot that Yéyé had appropriated many years before for him and Nǎinai was the perfect spot for his eternal rest. Once the casket had been lowered into the ground, we each took turns to throw a handful of earth onto it as we wished him well in the afterlife. Then we shared in prayers at his graveside. I couldn't help but feel cheated to have this amazing man taken from my life. I had always adored Yéyé, and I knew that I would continue to miss him terribly.

White envelopes containing money were then handed to us, and it was time to take our leave. As we turned away from the graveside, and with fresh tears coursing down my cheeks, I caught a glimpse of my golden balloon floating nearby in the sky. And behind it, for the briefest of moments, I thought that I saw the hazy outline of an old army plane just before it disappeared behind the clouds.

I smiled.

"Fly high, Yéyé, and fly free. I love you," I whispered as, with a heavy heart, I took my little sister's hand and led her back towards home.

Becoming Mei-Rose

Becoming Mei-Rose

自爱
Beetle Bugs and Bras

A major highlight of my senior year came in the fall—I had finally saved up enough money to buy my very own car. It was a beat up yellow Beetle, but I absolutely loved it. Wing came along with me to pick it up from the seller.

"*Aii-ya*, jiějiě, she's a beauty!" he said, running his hand along the bodywork. "A little rusty in places, but I can help you to patch her up!" He grinned at me. "And it'll be nice not having to get the bus to school anymore! I call shotgun!"

"You'll need to take that up with Ling," I laughed.

Wing chuckled as he got into the passenger seat. "Or maybe you can let *me* drive it to school, and then you and Ling can sort out who's sitting where!"

Grinning, I just rolled my eyes at him as I turned the key in the ignition, and my little yellow Bug roared into life.

爱

By Easter of that final school year, life felt pretty good. I still missed Matthew, but he was in his second year at college now, wherever he had gone. So, I tried to put him to the back of my mind and deal with the things that I did have control over, such as continuing to protect my wellbeing from my nemesis, Kendal.

One morning, as Wing, Ling and I pulled into St. Clement's parking lot, we saw lots of teenagers crowding around the hood of a bright red sports car. Parking the Bug nearby, Wing and I then got out, and I pulled my seat forward to let Ling climb out from the back.

"I mean," said an all-too-familiar shrill voice, "Daddy practically threw it at me! Said that only the best would do for his gorgeous princess."

The rising volume of her voice let my siblings and I know that we had been spotted and that this show was now for my benefit.

"Don't let her get to you," Wing said as he placed his hand on my arm.

"Oh, don't worry," I said. "It's been a long time now since she got under my skin. I think that's what bothers her the most!"

We watched as the crowd parted to reveal Kendal sitting on the hood of a brand new Porsche, twirling its key around her index finger. She was managing an expression of smugness mixed with malice, which made her look like she had tasted something unpleasant. She stood up and took a few steps towards us.

"Did *your* daddy buy you that heap of junk over there?" she asked with feigned innocence, looking at my car behind us. "Oh, what a shame that's all he could afford. Or maybe you're just not worth spending money on!"

I felt Ling flinch next to me, so I took her hand in mine to reassure her that I was okay.

"Yet again, you are so wrong, Kendal," I replied calmly. "I bought my own car, and I love it, so I don't care what you or anyone else has to say about it. That car represents all of my own hard work ... that I can do these things for myself. Why should my father buy me stuff like that when he has put a roof over my head and food in my stomach for the last 17 years? He has given me more than enough, and I am grateful that I have been shown how to stand on my own two feet!

"But, don't spend time worrying about me. Go and enjoy your car. It certainly is pretty. However, I'm sure you'll be begging your father to get you another one soon enough once you get bored of its color!"

Some of the teenagers surrounding Kendal snickered, and she silenced them with one glare before she turned back to glower at me.

"*Woah*, girl!" said Filipa, who had come to stand next to Wing while I had said my piece. "You tell her!"

We all laughed and turned towards the school's entrance, but then sudden shouts and screams halted our retreat and we turned back around to stare mayhem in the face. Teenagers were running in all directions to get out of the way of a white car that was careering into the parking lot. We stood open-mouthed and watched as it headed straight for Kendal's new Porsche … and Kendal.

Wing didn't hesitate, and he raced to where Kendal was seemingly rooted to the spot, staring at the oncoming vehicle in undisguised horror. Grabbing her around the waist, he tackled her out of the out-of-control car's path, and they both landed in a heap next to a nearby flowerbed.

It was just in the nick of time as the white car crashed into the Porsche seconds later, and the deafening sound ricocheted off the surrounding buildings. Kendal was oblivious to this, however, as she was too busy trying to shove my brother away from her.

"Get *off* me! What do you think you're doing? I said ... get *off*!" she shouted at Wing, so he untangled himself and stood up as anxious teachers came hurrying out of the school to see what had happened and to make sure that everyone was okay.

"Oh! My car!" Kendal screamed as she scrambled to her feet and looked upon the mangled mess that had, only moments before, been her gloating glory. As she stared in disbelief at it, its front bumper creaked and fell to the ground, making her scream once more in agitation, her hands clenched at her side.

Wing came back to stand with us, and I quickly fussed over him to make sure that he was okay. Apart from a few superficial scratches, he seemed unharmed.

We then watched as the teachers pulled William Austin from the white car. He seemed dazed, though fortunately conscious, and he had a deep cut above his left eye where he must have hit his head on the steering wheel.

"My br—brakes," he said. "My brakes w—w—wouldn't work!"

"You idiot!" screamed Kendal as she came storming up to where he sat on the ground and towered over him. "Look! Look at what you did to my car! Wait 'til my father hears about this! He'll sue you for every dime that you have!" Her voice had risen so high that it was almost a screech.

The athletics coach, who had been one of the first teachers on the scene, pulled Kendal back by the arm and looked at her with disgust.

"Kendal Johnson. Austin has received a nasty head injury, so he will not benefit from you screaming at him like a banshee! Please be quiet, and we will sort all of this out in due course." Kendal looked as if she was going to say something else, but the coach was having none of it. "I mean it Ms. Johnson. Not another word!"

As Kendal stomped towards us, furiously shaking off her friends' attempts to comfort her, Filipa barred her way. My friend started to laugh, although it didn't quite reach her eyes, and she stood defiantly with one hand on her hip. "Karma's a bitch, huh?" she said, smirking as she raised an eyebrow. Kendal just glared at her.

Then Filipa stood to one side, and as Kendal pushed by us all, we noticed her eyes linger briefly on Wing. But without another word, she disappeared into school.

Wing's friend, Tony, came up to us and patted my brother on the shoulder. "Good save, Wyatt! But if I had been you, I'd have left her where she stood!"

"Tony!" I said, shocked.

"I'm only joking, Rose, don't worry! But seriously ... did she even thank you, buddy?"

Wing shrugged and laughed. "This is Kendal Johnson we are talking about! Of course she didn't! But thank goodness William looks like he'll be okay ..."

The boys went off chatting as the bell for morning classes rang inside the building. Filipa and I waved to Ling, who ran off to join her friends heading into school, and we turned in the direction of the calculus block.

"Didn't I tell you so?" Filipa said.

I turned to her and raised my eyebrows in confusion. "Tell me what?"

"What goes around comes around, of course!" she grinned at me.

I chuckled and gave her a friendly shove. "Yes, you did, oh wise one! Come on ... or we'll be late, and we've got that test today!"

Filipa groaned as she tucked her arm in mine, but I smiled as I felt the lightest of touches on my opposite shoulder. Out of the corner of my eye, I could see my golden balloon bobbing right behind me—I had done well, and I knew it, yet here it was to validate it too, just in case.

I raised my hand as if to tuck my hair

behind my ear, but instead I reached beyond. To my utter joy, the balloon let me brush it with my fingertips, and I felt a warm fluttering inside my chest. I breathed a deep, contented sigh. I felt so happy. Happy and strong.

爱

Soon it was May, and Māmā and Bàba were so proud of my marks in the final SAT exams that they had agreed to let me go to my senior prom. Māmā had even agreed to finance my dress for me, although the shoes were down to me to buy.

So, three weeks before the event, we visited a boutique dress shop where I knew Filipa had purchased her own gown. A little bell tinkled as we opened the door, reminding me instantly of Auntie Bunty and my second home—I became excited at the thought of telling her all about the dress that I would get.

Māmā and I began rooting through the plethora of fancy dresses on the racks. Straight away, I could tell that my mother wasn't happy, and she started complaining to me as soon as she held up a dress to show me.

"This is not appropriate, gūniáng!" she said in Cantonese, looking most indignant.

"Where are the sleeves? And the chest is nearly bare! What would that cover? It doesn't even have straps, so how will it stay up?"

At that moment, the sales assistant came over to help us, and even though it was obvious that she didn't understand what my mother was saying, Māmā's tone was very clear to interpret.

"Māmā, please ..." I said, smiling at the waiting sales assistant. "Let's see what is here?"

"I don't see why Auntie Lian can't just make you a dress!" my mother continued in Cantonese, ignoring the lady standing patiently next to us. "Hers are always appropriate for young women to wear!"

"Māmā," I tried again. "We agreed that I could look at dresses in a shop like all of my friends. Let the lady help us?"

Finally facing the sales assistant, my mother stared up at her and thrust the dress in her face as she spoke in her broken English. "This dress wedding dress. No need wedding dress. Need prom dress. With sleeves!"

"Māmā, I would like a sleeveless dress, as all of my friends will be wearing dresses without sleeves."

"But you will get cold!"

"Māmā, it will be fine," I reassured her. I turned to the sales assistant and smiled. "Please can you help me to find something that will suit me? I'm not curvy at all, I'm afraid, so I don't know what will suit my figure?"

"You have a lovely figure, my dear," gushed the sales assistant. "And please, call me Daphne."

So, Daphne got to work pulling prom dresses from the rack as Māmā's lips became more and more pursed. It took all of my persuading to stop her from walking out of the shop, and eventually she accepted that one of the strapless dresses did look quite pretty on me. It was made from soft white lace with a black fabric belt, and its skirt was ruffled and layered. It was beautiful!

"But you wear a shawl!" Māmā said in a tone that made it quite clear that there was no compromise to be made.

"Okay, Māmā. If that will make you happy," I said as I smiled at her.

"Happier. Not happy," she grumbled.

Once we had finalized our choice and set up a date for my fitting, Daphne very patiently explained to my mother how the top part of the dress could be trusted to do its job, even without straps, and that a bra was stitched into it to ensure that everything remained decent.

Poor Daphne! The look that Māmā gave

her would have made a toughened soldier crack, but she just remained smiling pleasantly until my mother completed her scrutiny and nodded once at her.

"Thank you. Goodbye," Māmā said brusquely as she turned to leave the shop.

"Thank you so much, and I'll see you next week," I said to Daphne as I hurried after my mother. I was so excited!

爱

By the time it came to my fitting, Auntie Lian had managed to convince Māmā that my dress was going to be perfect for a prom. She had even shown her the photos of Ju in her prom dress—so similar to mine, except that it had been black with a white belt.

Once Māmā had paid for the dress and its alterations, Daphne helped me to choose the perfect shoes to go with it. She was very impressed that I was paying for these using my own money, which made Māmā warm more to her immediately.

"Not a bad lesson for youngsters today," Daphne said as I handed over my hard-earned cash. "Too many expect their parents to get them everything they need, don't they?"

爱

The next day at school, I told Filipa that I was all set, and that I had my dress and shoes all ready to go.

"So, who are you going with?" Filipa said.

"*Errr* ... pardon?"

"Oh Rose! Who is going to be your date?"

"My date?" I squealed. "I can't have a date! There's no way my parents would let me go if it was a date! I was just going to tag along with you!"

"As much as I adore you, Rose, you are *not* going to be a spare wheel on my date with Ben!" Filipa laughed. "You'll need to think of someone to ask who your parents will approve of."

"Well ... the only boy my parents would approve of is Wyatt. They know I'll be safe with him ... what do you think?"

"Your brother? You can't take your brother to the prom!" Filipa said as she rolled her eyes in despair. "*Argh!* You are hopeless!"

"Well, what about Tony, then? He's Wyatt's best friend, so they might be okay with me going with him?"

"Do you know if he's been asked already? Someone might have beaten you to it!"

"Oh ... I don't know."

"Well, I guess you better go and find out!" said Filipa. "Go on! Off you go!"

And so, cheeks burning, I went off to find my brother and Tony.

I found them by the basketball courts, chatting to other friends. Wing gave me a big smile and a wave as I approached.

"Hi, jiějiě! You looking for me?"

"*Errrr* ... no, actually. I ... *errrr* ... need to speak to Tony."

Wing frowned at me as he got Tony's attention. Thankfully, the other friends said their goodbyes and wandered off—I already wanted the ground to open up and swallow me whole without having an audience to witness my embarrassment.

"Hi, Rose. You good?" Tony said as Wing crossed his arms and watched the exchange with a puzzled expression.

"Yes, Tony, I'm ... *errrr* ... great. I was wondering though if you could do me ... *errrr* ... a favor? That's if you can, I mean. Because, obviously, if you can't, then that's fine too."

As Tony's expression changed to one of confusion, Wing's changed to one of understanding. His whole face lit up and he grinned. "Oh, this should be good!" he said as I glared at him.

"Eh?" said Tony.

I took a deep breath. "Tony. Please will you come to the prom with me?" Tony grinned as Wing started to laugh. "Quiet!" I berated my brother as I looked back at Tony, my cheeks feeling as though they were on fire.

"Rose," Tony began with a smirk, "I didn't know that you felt that way. I'm flattered!"

"Oh, shush! You know that I don't!" I huffed as my brother fell about laughing. "But I need someone to take me to the prom, and I thought you'd be the best choice *because* you know it's not like *that*."

"Best offer you'll get today, buddy," Wing said between snorts.

Tony grinned at me and said, "Of course I'll take you, Rose. I'd be honored to. But please … no hanky-panky!"

"Oh!" I threw my hands up, exasperated. "Behave!"

爱

The day of the prom arrived, and despite her

reservations, Māmā was getting caught up in the excitement of it too. She had invited Auntie Lian and Ju around to help me to get ready, which was perfect—I knew nothing about hair and make-up, and Māmā knew even less.

As I sat there with my robe on, being pampered and groomed, I laughed as a realization dawned.

"This will be you soon, Ju! Not long to go until your wedding now! I suppose prom is almost like a trial run!"

Make-up done, Auntie Lian then began with my hair. She had already put it in curlers, and now she created a beautifully crafted pile of curls atop my head with some locks hanging delicately down. She sprayed them in place without warning me to close my mouth, and I was soon coughing and spluttering as I choked on the hairspray.

"Careful," she warned, "or you'll ruin your makeup!"

"*Aiii-yaa*! What is that stuff?" I said as Ju laughed.

"It will keep your hair looking pretty all night, so close your mouth and let me finish fixing it in place!"

This time prepared, I held my breath as I was enveloped in more sticky mist. Once this torture was over, the end result was very becoming—even I was pleasantly surprised as I looked at myself in the mirror. Now it was time to get my dress and shoes on.

But, before I could get the dress over my head, Māmā came into the room holding a strapless bra aloft.

"Děngdài! Wait! She must put this on!" she said.

"Chu Hua, it's fine," Auntie Lian said. "Remember, there is already a bra sewn in, so nothing will fall out!"

"No," my mother insisted. "She will wear this, or she will not go out at all!"

Auntie Lian smiled at me as Māmā gave me the bra and waited for me to put it on. Once I had, she then stepped back and waited for Auntie Lian and Ju to help me put my dress on without spoiling my hair. The extra bra now made my chest very tight, as well as giving it somewhat of a lift, and I found it hard to breathe.

"*Aiii-ya*! What have you got in there?" Ling said as she walked into the room and pointed at my chest. "You are twice the size!"

"Lee Ling, hush!" scolded my mother. "At least nothing can fall out and ruin her dignity!"

As my mother left the room to go and find the camera, Auntie Lian squeezed my arm.

"Here is a clutch bag, Mei. When you arrive at the dance, visit the restroom and remove the extra bra ... put it in the bag. Or otherwise I fear that you will run out of oxygen!"

Māmā returned with the camera and the buttonhole that I had bought for Tony's suit. On the chime of 7 o'clock, the doorbell rang and Bàba opened the door to find Tony standing on the doorstep. Wing's friend looked very smart in his black and white tuxedo.

"Oh, thank goodness," he said when he looked at my dress. "My mom gave me so much grief because I had forgotten to ask you what color your dress was. Apparently we have to match, or something? So, I guess we lucked out!"

Then he looked at me properly for the first time. "And wow, Rose! You look stunning!"

My father coughed, and Tony put his hands up in defense. "I mean that with the greatest of respect, Mr. Lee."

Wing slapped Tony on the back and laughed, but then his tone became more serious. "Look after my sister, buddy. I'm trusting you."

"Of course!" Tony said, handing me my corsage—a floral wrist band boasting the most beautiful white rose set against dark green leaves and peppered with little red blossoms.

The Origami Balloon

And then we had to pose for the endless obligatory photographs before my mother wrapped a black lace shawl firmly around my bare shoulders. Everyone laughed.

For the first time in my life, I felt beautiful. And that feeling lasted for the whole night as Tony proved to be the most perfect gentleman. We danced and chatted with Filipa and Ben, and I honestly didn't want the evening to end. It felt like the fairytale that Ju was always talking about, and it *was* almost perfect. Almost.

As Tony walked me back to the car where Wing was waiting for me, he kissed me on the cheek.

"Thank you for asking me to the prom, Rose. I am honored to have been your date tonight, and all I can say is that the person you choose one day to be your *real* date will be one hell of a lucky guy."

As I blushed, he waved at Wing through the windscreen and sauntered off to find where his own mother was waiting in her car to take him home.

I flopped into the passenger seat as Wing turned to look at me. "Good night?" he asked.

"The best! But I'm exhausted. Take me home please, dìdì."

"You bet. And he's right, you know?"

"Who?" I said as Wing started the engine.

"Tony. I can't wait to meet the guy lucky enough to get to marry you. Love you, jiějiě."

But I couldn't answer due to the lump in my throat. Instead, I grabbed my brother's nearest wrist on the steering wheel and gave it a squeeze as I looked across at him with a warm, watery smile full of love.

自爱

Coincidences

As I placed the last bag on the back seat of my Beetle, a lump formed in my throat. Shutting the door, I leaned back against it and looked up at my childhood home in front of me. The home I was now moving out of as I began the next chapter of my life: college.

With Auntie Bunty's encouragement, I had signed up for a catering course at the Institute of Culinary Education in New York. I was following my passion! But, I was terrified. Having lived in the Midwest of America for my entire life, I was now going to be living, for the next three years at least, all the way over in the North-East. And it was going to take me 15 hours to drive there, which was a long way to be from my family. I considered this thought and shuddered.

I closed my eyes and took several deep breaths, and I reminded myself that I could do this. I had to do this. I had decided months ago that if I wanted any chance of proving to myself that I was capable of being truly independent, then there was no other choice but to put substantial distance between me and my loved ones. This would stop me from running home at the drop of a hat, and it would force me to stand on my own two feet and figure things out for myself.

"Jiějiě? You okay?"

Wing and Ling had come down the front steps, and they turned to lean back against my car too, either side of me. They looked sad, so I took their hands in mine and gave them a squeeze.

"I'm fine, dìdì," I said. "I guess it's just hitting me now how far away I'll be from you guys. But I'm excited for the adventure ahead too!"

"Our room will be weird without you," said Ling. "I don't know if I'll be able to sleep in there on my own."

"You'll get used to it, mèimei," I said as I smiled at her. "I'll need to adjust as well. I'm used to hearing your snores all night long!"

"*Aiiii-ya*! I don't snore!" she said, giving my side a little shove with her elbow, but then she smiled and wrapped both her arms around my waist and laid her head on my shoulder. "I'll miss you, jiějiě."

I kissed her forehead. "I'll miss you too.

Both of you," I said as I looked across at Wing. He gave me a grin and there was a mischievous twinkle in his eye.

"I'll miss the Bug more," he laughed. "Whose car can I borrow now to take me where I want to go?"

"You'll have to save up and buy your own. Maybe you'll actually put gas in that one!" I chuckled.

Wing grinned at me for a second, but then he looked solemn again. "You *are* coming back home in two weeks though, aren't you?" he said. "For the Moon Festival? Is that for definite?"

"Absolutely! I wouldn't miss that for the world. And you know that my mooncakes rival even those of Năinai now!" I laughed. "I can't have you missing out on those."

My siblings laughed as Māmā and Bàba came down the steps towards us.

"All set, Mei?" asked Bàba.

"Yes, I think so. If I've forgotten anything, I can always pick it up in a fortnight when I come home again."

Māmā handed me a flask. "Soup. For the journey. Ching Po Leung herb pork bone," she said as I went to open the flask to see. "Keep it closed or it'll get cold."

"Thank you, Māmā," I said as I felt tears

sting my eyes. I knew that my mother appeared to the outside world as a stern individual who seemed to be permanently serious, but she had always had her own way of showing us her love—usually in the form of the time she spent with us, teaching us about our Chinese heritage, or in the form of countless flasks of soup over the years for every kind of ailment imaginable.

I opened the car door and tucked the flask next to the bags on the passenger seat. As I turned to face my family once more, I took a mental photograph of them standing there in that moment. My family, whom I loved so very much.

But now it was time to fly the nest and take my first steps out into the world on my own, and that was exciting; I knew that there would always be a place for me here. But, Māmā and Bàba had been preparing me for this day my whole life, and suddenly I realized that the terror had gone. It had been replaced by a calm certainty that everything was going to be okay.

"Right then," I said, feeling a little awkward. "I'll phone you when I get there, and I'll see you in two weeks!"

Māmā and Bàba stepped forward to embrace me, and they each kissed me on the cheek. Then I turned to face my siblings. Ling wasn't even trying to hide her tears, and Wing was standing with his hands in his pockets, staring miserably at the ground and kicking at a pebble.

"Don't cry, mèimei," I said as I pulled her into a hug. "You'll see ... two weeks will pass by really quickly, and I'll phone loads. I promise!"

Ling just sniffed loudly and then went to stand next to Māmā. Wing came over next and gave me a bear hug. "Don't worry, jiějiě," he whispered. "I'll make sure she's okay."

I nodded at him in gratitude and smiled before getting into my car. Winding down the window, I started the ignition and beamed up at them all. No more words were needed. As I pulled out from the curb, my family moved forwards as one, Wing with his arm around Ling's shoulders. Looking in my rear-view mirror, I could see them all waving me off, so I honked my horn and laughed as I saw Māmā tut and shake her head at my audacity. Then I stuck my arm out of my open window and waved until I rounded a bend in the street and they were lost from sight.

The next couple of weeks were spent frantically

signing up for the right classes and trying not to get lost on the subway. New York was huge, and it had such a great vibe. I loved it.

My apartment in Chinatown was small, but clean and comfortable, and it wasn't far from my college. My roommate was lovely: a Canadian girl who had traveled from Toronto to join the elite culinary program in New York, and we bonded instantly through our shared loves of cooking and books. Sophie's passion was French cuisine, but she was genuinely interested in learning more about Chinese food too. We enjoyed swapping menus and cooking for each other when we weren't at college.

The others in my class were all so easy to be around too. From the start, there was a healthy respect for what everyone brought to the table, so to speak. There were no cliques, and no divides. We were one team, and it felt so refreshing. My peers were as intrigued by my culture as I was by theirs—in our class we had several Americans and Canadians, but we also had a Scot, three Romanians, a Hungarian, two Africans, four Indians, an Australian and a Russian. So much diversity!

Soon, it was time to return home for the Moon Festival. But, before I left, my tutors and classmates were desperate to know more about this custom, so I was invited to teach them all how to make mooncakes—an honor indeed. So, I rolled up my sleeves and led my first class at culinary school.

To make the dough, I sourced golden syrup, lye water and vegetable oil and mixed them all together. Then I sieved plain flour into the mixture. At first, it was a sticky mess, but after plenty of mixing, it became a lovely soft dough. Then I wrapped it in cling wrap and put it in the fridge to cool and relax for half an hour.

Next, I showed them how to make the lotus seed paste for the filling. To remove the lotus seed skins, I boiled the seeds in water for 10 minutes. I explained that I had added some alkaline water to the boiling water too—this would make the skin soft enough to peel off.

Once the seeds had been boiled enough, I began the lengthy job of removing the skins, but fortunately I had plenty of volunteers to help me—this was always a job that I roped Ling into helping me with at home.

Once all the skins had been removed, I boiled the seeds again until they were soft. I let them cool while I removed my dough from the fridge and checked it. Then I popped the seeds into a food processor to puree them. It was now time to create the paste.

Putting a wok on a low heat, I added groundnut oil and sugar. Once the sugar had dissolved and turned golden, I added the lotus seed puree and more sugar. I liked my mooncakes sweet, so I always added plenty of sugar, and I explained to my peers that they could adjust the sweetness at this point to accommodate personal tastes.

I continued to stir fry the paste until it became nearly dry, and then I added oil and stirred, repeating this until the paste had become thick. Lastly, I added in the maltose, and I kept stirring until the paste left the sides of the wok. I removed it from the heat and left it to cool.

Next, I showed the class how to add the filling to a small ball of dough, making sure that the dough was not too thick in places—the perfect mooncake had a consistent depth all the way around, and this was something that I prided myself on. I then rolled the mooncakes in a bowl of flour and then popped them one-by-one into my mooncake mold that I had brought in that day especially; this gave the mooncakes their familiar pattern and shape.

Finally, it was time to bake the cakes, and I put them in the oven for five minutes to allow them to firm up before taking them out again and applying some egg-wash to them—this would help the mooncakes to turn a lovely golden brown. I grinned at my classmates as I put the cakes back in the oven to finish cooking.

"Just enough time to get washed up, and I'll make some Chinese tea for us to drink with our mooncakes!"

Fifteen minutes later, I was being applauded for my culinary genius as everyone tucked into their sweet treats. The tutors were very impressed by the taste that I had created, and they asked if they could have the recipe. I wished that my family and Auntie Bunty could have seen me in that moment—I was sure that they would have been proud of me.

I explained to everyone that Chinese people celebrated the Moon Festival each year to thank the moon for the bountiful harvest at the end of autumn. I told them to visit Chinatown during the upcoming festival to see the lanterns of all shapes and sizes being carried and displayed; symbolic beacons to light everyone's path to good fortune and prosperity. And then I came to my favorite part of the festival: introducing the story of Chang'e, the moon goddess.

I paused momentarily as this triggered a painful memory from my past: an insecure young girl at middle school, alone in the restroom stall, imagining her own escape to the moon as Chang'e had done. How things had changed for me since that day. And if only it were possible to have five minutes with my younger self; I could have reassured her that everything would be fine in the end.

A nervous cough brought me out of my reverie, and I saw that everyone in the room was looking at me in concern.

"Oh sorry! I was just remembering something. Anyway, Chang'e …" and I transported my peers to the wonderful oriental world of Chinese myth and legend.

Towards the end of the session, and as I looked around the room, my golden balloon bobbed into view and settled behind my shoulder. I sensed warmth and peace emanating from it, and I breathed a contented sigh. Tomorrow I would be making the journey home to see everyone and to celebrate the Moon Festival with them all. Life was good. It was very, very good.

Sophie caught my eye from across the room, grinned and gave me a thumbs up as she took another bite of her second mooncake. I felt myself blush, but that was okay … I knew now that it was just a part of who I was. And that was good enough for me.

爱

Months later, I had settled really well into New York City life. During the holidays, I still went home and worked with Auntie Bunty in the café, so I felt like I had the best of both worlds.

During term, I spent my evenings and weekends—when I wasn't expected to be in class—partaking in study groups or reading in the local library. My parents had made it quite clear that I wasn't to even consider dating until after my college years, and that was fine by me. My heart wouldn't have been in it anyway. I watched Sophie get ready most weekends for her dates, but I knew that this wasn't really my scene, so off to the library I would go if I felt the need to get out of the apartment.

One Friday evening, I sat curled up in one of the library armchairs, reading a book about Persian mythology, when my focus was interrupted by a familiar voice. A voice from the past that made my heart stop and my body sink further into the chair. I pulled the book up over my face.

"No ... honestly. The lecturer today said that Ötzi the Iceman might have been part of a ritual sacrifice, and not killed in a raiding party

attack," said the voice that I knew.

"Is that the mummy they found on the Austrian and Italian border?" asked a female voice.

"Yes ..."

And so the conversation continued, but I heard no more as I frantically tried to work out what to do. Most of me wanted to stay hidden, but the core of me ached to make my presence known.

I peeked over my book and watched as Matthew and the girl continued to walk past me towards a nearby table. They were still talking as they sat down, although now their voices were too faint to make out what they were saying. I saw that Matthew's female friend was choosing the chair where she would have her back to me. And as Matthew sat opposite her, I realized that I would be in his line of vision.

Something whacked me on the head.

"*Aiii-ya*! Stop that! I know ... I know ..." I whispered to my golden balloon. "I *am* going to be brave!"

So, as my balloon took up its normal position behind me, I sat up straight in the chair and placed the book in my lap. Then I looked at Matthew, willing him to look my way.

It didn't take long. I was just wondering

where he had reached in his Ötzi the Iceman story when he glanced over and caught my eye. His whole body stiffened, and his mouth dropped open. His friend looked over her shoulder, looking for the distraction that had stalled her companion. Her eyes travelled over me but did not stop, and she turned back to Matthew. He put his hand up in apology, and then he gestured towards me as he rose from his seat.

My stomach churned as he approached, but I willed myself not to look down. I maintained his eye-contact for the entire time, smiling at him to still my nerves.

"Rose? Is that really you? What are you doing here?" he said, his face unreadable.

"Hi Matthew. It's been some time, huh?" I said, hoping the tremor in my voice wasn't noticeable. "I started college this year ... at the Institute of Culinary Education actually. I didn't know that you had come to New York. Where are you studying?"

Matthew regarded me before answering. "I'm at NYU studying archeology."

"Well ... that makes sense after all of those books you read on Ancient Egypt!" I laughed, but Matthew just raised an eyebrow.

Next came an awkward silence. I glanced

over to where Matthew's friend had twisted around in her seat, watching our exchange, so I gave her a little smile. She raised her hand to wave hello.

"Look, Matthew," I began as he continued to stare at me in silence, stony-faced. "I owe you a massive apology."

"You owe me nothing ... don't worry about it."

"No ... please. I really do. When you asked me to—"

"I said, it's fine," Matthew interrupted. "It's all water under the bridge ... ancient history."

"But, that's just it," I said. "I don't want it to be. What happened in the library that day was all about me ... not you. You did nothing wrong, but my—my own ... *errr* ... insecurities stopped me from accepting your invitation. I wanted to say yes! Really I did!"

"Oh, that old chestnut! It wasn't you ... it was me?" he snorted.

"Please, Matthew. I was scared!"

"Scared of me?"

"No ... scared that—"

"What, Rose? What could you have possibly been scared of?"

"*Aiiii-ya!*" I said, throwing my arms up. "I

was scared that you'd ask me and then realize that you had made a huge mistake. Okay?"

Matthew continued to stare at me as if processing what I had just said. "Well," he finally muttered, "I guess we'll never know now, will we? Look. It's been great seeing you and everything, but me and Jilly are off to see a movie, so I have to go."

"Sure," I mumbled. "It was really great seeing you too."

And I sat there watching as Matthew went to collect Jilly, and then he walked out of my life once again.

爱

After that day, I established a habit of visiting the library every Friday night and curling up in the same armchair with a good book. I was under no illusion that I would see Matthew again, but it felt safe to carry on the same routine that I had established at home in the library there, plus it was now the last time and place that I had seen him.

So, it came as a great surprise when, two months later, Matthew flopped down in the armchair opposite me, interrupting my literary adventure.

"So ... let me get this straight," he said with no preamble. "You said no to my invitation, looked horrified at the very thought of attending prom with me and then laughed in my face, not because you thought my idea was ridiculous, but because you didn't think that you deserved my attention?"

"That seems ... *errr* ... pretty accurate," I managed.

"And you couldn't have just told me that?"

"No ... it appears not."

"What you don't realize is that it took me a long time to get over you," he said as he looked at his hands. "I didn't even *go* to the prom in the end. Because there was no one else I wanted to go with."

"Oh, I'm—"

"No ... I don't need you to say sorry again. I heard you the first time. What I need to know is where you think we go from here. Because I'm going to be honest with you. I don't want to be 'just friends' with you. But I'm also not going to open up my heart to you if you are just going to hurt it again."

"Matthew ... I'm not the same Rose as I was then, I promise. All I can do is prove it to you over time."

Matthew leaned forward and stared into my eyes. My thoughts became jumbled as I realized that he really was the most beautiful soul that I had ever met. I held my breath.

"Right then. Prove it," he said. "Prove to me that you love yourself first, and then …"

The meaning was clear as the unsaid words hovered in the air—his heart would remain locked to me until I could prove that I was able to accept the love that he wanted to give. And, I realized, that was fair enough.

自爱
Mei-Rose

As I stood next to the window in my childhood bedroom, I gazed down upon the old green ash tree outside in the back yard. Its leaves were silvery in the moonlight, like burnished pewter. I watched as its branches swayed in the light breeze, dancing to their own secret melody.

My eyes drifted to the rose bush beneath the tree, and my heart faltered as I remembered for whom it had been planted. I raised my hand to press it against the pane, and I smiled a sad smile.

"*Ai-ya*, Ai. Will you look at me now?" I whispered. "All grown up, but a day still doesn't pass without me thinking of you, my friend. I wish you were still here."

Slim arms slipped around my waist from behind, and I felt Ling's head rest on the back of my shoulder.

"You really loved that dog, jiějiě," she said. "Where do you think he is now?"

"Hopefully, happily chasing his tail

beyond Rainbow Bridge and having the time of his life!" I said, twisting around in her arms and then wrapping both of mine around her too. I rested my cheek upon her head. "He was the best, mèimei. He loved me no matter what, and he taught me that I was worth something in this confusing world!"

We were silent for a moment as we reflected upon years long past. Then Ling pulled away and held me at arm's length.

"I love you, jiějiě. I just wanted to tell you that in case I don't get a chance to tell you tomorrow. It's going to be such a crazy day, but I need you to know that you are the best big sister anyone could have ever wished for. I mean it! You have always been there for me and protected me. You and Wing ... you're my best friends. How lucky I am that you are my family too!"

I pulled Ling back into a hug and squeezed her hard.

"And you know how much I love you, mèimei. You and Wing have always been there for me too, despite all of my idiosyncrasies over the years! *Aiiii-ya*! I cringe now, looking back!"

"Don't you dare cringe!" Ling said. "That's part of your journey, and part of you becoming who you are today. I'm super proud of you!"

"Bed ... both of you!" Māmā said as she

came into the room and turned down our sheets. "You need your sleep tonight, and it's already late, so no more chattering or you will look haggard in the morning, and that won't do!"

"Yes, Māmā," we chorused as Ling got into her bed after giving me one last squeeze. I sat on the edge of my bed and smiled as I watched my mother tuck my sister in as though she were still a child.

"And you," Māmā gestured to me. "Get into bed and let your old māmā tuck you in one last time ..."

Ever biddable, I did as she asked, and she began to fuss with the sheets, bringing them up to tuck underneath my chin.

"Māmā?" I said.

"Yes, gūniáng?" she answered as she continued to tug at my sheets.

"I love you."

My mother stopped and looked at me in surprise. We weren't ones for open expressions of love like this. But, I needed her to hear it. I watched as her face relaxed and a little smile played upon it. Then she bent down and patted my cheek gently.

"Good ... good. That is good," she murmured before kissing my forehead lightly. "Now sleep!" And with that, she bustled out of the room.

Within moments, the deep breathing coming from the other side of the room let me know that Ling was already asleep. It was no wonder really after the previous two days of family gatherings and feasting. This evening, it had already been well past midnight when Wing had finally claimed victory in our game of Mahjong. Some things would never change!

But I couldn't sleep. My mind was buzzing for what the next day would bring, and so I unraveled myself from my sheets and walked to the window once more. The floorboards felt cool under my bare feet, and I gave a little shiver underneath the cotton of my nightdress. Fall had most certainly arrived.

As I gazed up at the moon, Chang'e came to mind, and I chuckled softly as I remembered how I had once wished for someone to love me as much as Hou Yi had loved her. Now I knew the truth: in order to have someone love you with such depth and fire, you had to love yourself in that way too. That was the secret, and only then could you welcome in the person who *deserved* your love and who would love you as you should be loved. And by doing just that, I had certainly found my Hou Yi.

In the window's reflection, I saw my

golden balloon bobbing behind me, so I smiled and turned around to face it. It was hovering in the center of the room, right in the path of the moonlight streaming in through the gap in the curtains. I took a couple of steps towards it and then reached out to it, palms up.

Ever so slowly, the balloon glided towards me and came to rest upon my hands. It was so shiny, and I could see my reflection upon its surface; my face was lit up, radiating pure happiness.

"Did Ai send you to me, I wonder?" I said, feeling in awe of the fact that I was being allowed to hold my golden companion properly for the first time.

In reply, and with some fleeting disappointment on my part, the balloon lifted up ever so slightly and began to glow. As I watched, transfixed, its origami design began to unfold as golden light began to pour out from its openings. Before long, I was so immersed in light that I couldn't see the darkened room beyond. The balloon had unfolded into a much larger heart shape, upon which moving, silent images flickered like they did on an old, grainy 1920s movie reel.

I peered more closely and caught my breath as I realized that these images were all of

The Origami Balloon

me and my family. There I was aged three, playing in the tub with a chubby two-year-old Wing. And there … I was pedaling as fast as I could in the sunny back yard on my little purple tricycle while a baby Ling sat in her pram, clapping her hands in delight.

Images appeared of me with Māmā and then with Bàba. Ju and I laughing as we played hide and seek. Yéyé tickling me as I sat on his knee while Năinai scolded him for making me giggle like a hyena. Me standing in Năinai's kitchen, covered in coconut flour while helping her to cook …

And so they kept coming. Each time an image was replaced by another, it would float up to circle above my head as it continued playing on a loop.

Then I reached a hand towards the heart-shaped screen as I felt the familiar ache inside my chest. "Oh, Ai," I whispered sadly, watching the image play out of a scruffy dog with his tongue lolling out of his mouth and his tail wagging furiously. I was throwing his ball for him, and I must have been about five years old.

Every time he brought it back, he placed it in my hand with such gentleness and then gave my face a lick.

I felt the tears trickle down my cheeks as I watched the image float up to the ceiling; I wasn't ready to stop watching that one just yet.

Next came the memory of little Ling crying as she fed the steamed buns to the ducks in the park. She had been so headstrong in those days. But I felt proud as I watched six-year-old me manage my little sister's behavior, and I smiled as I watched grumpy Ling stomp back to where Wing and our mother were waiting for us.

And then appeared a girl I could barely remember as I hadn't seen her for so long, but there was beautiful Bethany with her lovely braids, showing me around the kindergarten classroom. My friends were claiming their place in my silent movie too it would appear.

"*Aiiii-ya!*" I laughed as a seven-year-old Filipa came into focus. The memory was of us holding hands and walking around the playground while I pointed things out to her and told her their English name. She had been small and wiry then, but it was still possible to see the fire in her soul.

On and on the movie clips played. I cringed when I saw myself hiding in the restroom, and how I had acted when Kendal had been mean. But then, I straightened my shoulders and raised my chin—I had learned to grow resilient in the end. My strength had always been in me, even back in middle school—I knew that now—but I just hadn't known how to harness it all those years ago.

Toronto, Florida, Washington D.C., San Francisco. Images of the family vacations flashed before my eyes. Ju and I excitedly sharing our motel room and gossiping into the night; Ling staring hopefully as we passed a pizza house on our way to yet another meal in a Chinese restaurant so that Yéyé could have his beloved rice.

I couldn't help the grin that spread across my face with the next image. There was dear Auntie Bunty standing over her spilled brownies the first day that I had met her—the day I had dug deep and found my courage to ask her for a job. That had been life-changing for me in so many different ways.

"*Ahhhhhhhhh,*" I breathed. "Matthew."

His face filled the balloon as the silent movie replayed a moment from our past. I watched as his eyebrows lifted, and his whole face became animated as he shared whatever it was that he was saying. His goodness radiated out of him like the brightest of auras, and I could see, now, how he *had* looked at me back then. Back when I had been unable to see it for myself.

There *was* adoration in those eyes, but I had been so blind to it at the time.

As I focused back on Matthew's image, I became aware that he was saying two words, over and over again, as though the movie reel had become scratched. "Love yourself."

I blushed as I remembered the many times that he had pushed my hand down from my mouth whenever I had tried to hide my braces; the times he had lifted my chin with a single finger as I had tried to hide behind my hair. "Love yourself."

"I do! I really, really do." I said, and I meant it. I loved the Chinese me, and I loved the American me. I loved that I wasn't the same as everyone else and that no one else had my eyes with their hazel flecks. I loved how I saw the world, and I loved how creative I was. And I really loved my imagination, which had allowed me an escape whenever the real world had become too much. Furthermore, I loved that these were my memories; wonderful memories of a rich and culturally diverse childhood. I loved that I was Mei *and* that I was Rose.

What I didn't love, however, was that I was a different identity to different people. That was the last hurdle I had to overcome, to address, but how could I change it? I remembered the day back in high school when Filipa had ordered me to look in the mirror and tell myself all of the things that I liked or disliked about myself. She had said then that I had to accept what I couldn't change, or change it if I could.

I gave a firm, resolute nod of my head as the answer clicked into place. "I love Mei, and I love Rose. But I need to be Mei-Rose," I told my balloon. "*Then* I will truly love myself just as I am."

As I said these words, Matthew's image floated up to the ceiling and joined the other ones orbiting around above me. The light surrounding me now glowed so brightly that I had to put a hand up to shield my eyes. The heart began to shrink and, as it did, it came closer and closer to my chest. The glare was so great that I had no option but to cover my eyes. However, I felt the contact the heart made; I felt my whole body fill up with love and warmth, from the very tips of my toes all the way up to the crown of my head. The space where I had previously felt only dull aches was now soothed and at peace, and I felt complete as I raised my hand to place it over my heart.

I opened my eyes to find myself standing alone, still in the center of the bedroom within the moonlit rays. In the shadows of the room, I could just about make out Ling sleeping without a care in the world, her chest rising and falling steadily. I grinned. My balloon was nowhere to be seen, but as I tingled inside, I knew that it would always be with me.

I tiptoed over to the window once more and looked down upon Ai's rosebush, and I blew it a kiss.

"I love you, Ai, and … thank you," I whispered into the night.

自爱
Please Drink Tea

The next day, I awoke to Ling bouncing on my bed. My eyes resisted being forced open as though I had only just fallen asleep moments before, but the sunlight blinding me let me know that morning had indeed arrived.

"Wake up, wake up, sleepyhead! Someone is getting married today!" Ling sang as she continued to bounce with relish.

"Get off my bed," I laughed, "before Māmā comes in and sees you! Then you'll be in trouble!"

Ling giggled but did as I said and only just in time as Māmā came into our room with my gold and red qixiong ruqun—my first outfit of the day. It was a breathtaking garment with its high waistline, heavily embroidered bodice and plethora of material lavishly draping from its sleeves.

"Breakfast is downstairs, but be quick," Māmā said. "We have much to do to get you ready, and Auntie Lian and Ju will be here soon to help you with your hair and makeup. Lái! Both of you!" And she flapped her arms at us to hurry up, making us feel as though we were a pair of errant hens getting under her feet.

Just as I was leaving the room, I glanced back to see Māmā laying my qixiong ruqun carefully upon the bed, smoothing out any wrinkles with her hand. But then she caught me watching her, and she shooed me out once more.

"I'm going," I laughed, and I ran down the stairs to catch up with Ling.

爱

Two hours later, I had my nose pressed up against the window in Wing's room, which overlooked the street outside. My hair had been pulled up into a duo ma ji—a bun that was gathered to one side of my head, and it had been peppered with jade-topped hairpins and artificial red berries. My qixiong ruqun flowed all around me, and I balanced on the one foot that wore my only bridal slipper, which had been sewn with exquisite golden thread like my bodice. My other foot was bare, save for the stocking that I was wearing.

Of course, I shouldn't have been at the window at all. Where I should have been was sitting on the chair in my room, waiting for my groom to come and find me. But, once I had heard the gongs ringing outside, I couldn't help but rush to see the spectacle down on the street.

Peering below, I could just make out the head of the procession. My groom looked very dashing as he led the way, holding the hand of Ju's and Huan's two-year-old son, Haoyu, who toddled next to him as a symbolic nod to fertility.

As the procession got nearer, I watched as Bàba, Wing and Uncle Bao walked towards the red and gold firecrackers that were hanging in the trees that were planted on the sidewalk in front of our house. This was such fun! As the fuses were lit, the men stood back and waited for the magic to happen.

Soon enough, loud cracking bangs echoed around the street, scaring away any evil spirits that may have been lurking, and the sparking showers of embers gave me such a child-like thrill. I saw little Haoyu point at them as he watched, open-mouthed, and smiling neighbors emerged from their homes to enjoy the show.

Once at the front door, the procession stopped, and Ling stepped forward looking very beautiful in her purple bridesmaid dress. I giggled as I waited for the chuangmen (door games) to begin.

"So," she said, a twinkle in her eye, "you believe you know all there is to know about your betrothed. Is this so?"

"I believe so," said Matthew, grinning at his soon-to-be-sister-in-law.

As this little exchange was taking place, Ju glanced up at Wing's window and winked at me—she knew me too well to think that I would have missed out on this hilarity. I beamed down at her as I remained poised, ready to retreat from sight if any other member of my family thought to look up.

"Well then," said Ling, clearly enjoying her task. "What is her favorite color?"

"Easy! Purple!" Matthew said.

"Favorite food?"

"Peking Roasted Duck!"

"Where is the place that she most wants to visit?"

"Are you even trying to challenge me?" Matthew laughed. "The Forbidden City, of course!"

"*Hmmmm* ... okay, let's think of a really tricky one," Ling said. "Favorite memory?"

"It was when you and Rose were little girls. You snuck out of the house when everyone else was asleep. You wanted to look at the stars, and Rose has always loved the moon. So, you both lay on the grass with Ai between you, and you talked about the possibility of other people out there in space, on a planet just like ours.

"Rose loved the wonderment that shone from your face and the fact that as she looked at you, she could see the stars reflected in your eyes. You soon fell asleep, so she told Ai about Chang'e as he lay with his head on her stomach. Just before the sun came up, she carried you back inside and up to bed."

Ling just looked at Matthew with the utmost respect, all traces of teasing now gone. Even I was blown away by the fact that he had remembered my childhood memory with such clear detail.

Refusing to look at Māmā—who had placed a hand on her hip and turned to look at my sister as soon as she had heard about us sneaking out of the house—Ling turned from Matthew to announce the beginning of the second chuangmen to the assembled crowd.

"And Ju, Filipa ... I need your help here please!"

My cousin and my friend, also looking stunning in their purple bridesmaid dresses, stepped forwards, Ju holding onto to Haoyu's hand.

"Here," Ju said to Matthew, "is a spicy chili pepper, a sweet egg bun, some bitter lemon peel and a sour gooseberry. You must eat all of them to show that you will be there for Mei throughout every stage of marriage. *Aiiii-ya*! No, érzi! That's not for you!" And everyone laughed as Ju rescued the chili pepper from Haoyu's hand.

"No," Ling laughed, "that pleasure is all Matthew's!"

I flinched as I watched my groom balk at the task ahead of him. But, he still reached forward and took each of the food items, glowering at Ling who was now in fits of laughter over his expression. Without pausing to over-think it, he stuffed in the chili first and crunched away before popping in the gooseberry and then the lemon peel. Slightly red in the face, he then began on the sweet egg bun—a sensible choice to leave to last.

Ling was nodding her head in approval as she, Filipa and Ju then took up position in front of the door, barring the way.

"There's more?" Matthew groaned.

"Oh, yes. I do believe that you came prepared with something to tempt us to surrender your bride to you?"

Matthew reached into his jacket pocket and removed a red packet. "You mean this?" he said as he waggled it in front of their faces while they grinned at him. "I think you'll find that there is enough in there to treat you three lovely ladies to a day at the spa!"

"Well, thank you," said Ju as she took it, and they all stepped out of the way. "Now, in order to claim your bride, you must first find her missing bridal shoe, and then you must find *her* in order to put it on her foot. Only then may you both attend the tea ceremony."

I giggled as I ran back to my room; it felt like the games of hide-and-seek that we had played as children in Nǎinai's and Yéyé's back yard. I thought that Matthew would know me well enough to figure out where I had hidden my shoe, so I couldn't wait to get to my own window to check and see if I was right.

Sure enough, I saw Matthew enter the back yard, and I watched with delight as he approached Ai's bush. Parting the rose stems with care, he reached in, and soon he found the missing shoe. He turned around and held it aloft with pride, the assembled audience cheering his discovery. Then, his eyes darted to my window, and I quickly flung myself behind my curtain as I laughed out loud.

"Go find your bride!" I heard Wing call out from below.

My heart was beating out of my chest by the time Matthew entered my bedroom to find me waiting for him, sitting on my chair as I should have been for the entire time. In his hand was my golden shoe, and his eyes lit up when he saw me in all of my finery.

"*Woah* ... Rose! You look like one of the Chinese princesses from your legends! You look amazing ... I mean, you ... *errr* ... always look amazing, but you look even more amazing today."

"Stop stalling and put *that* on my foot already," I laughed as my groom looked more flustered by the minute. "We've tea to serve!"

Matthew gave me a wonky smile as he knelt to put on my shoe. "Very Cinderella-like," he laughed. "Thank goodness it fits!"

Then, nerves forgotten, he swept me up into his arms as if I weighed no more than a feather and carried me out of my room and down the stairs to where our families were waiting for us in the living-room.

On the rosewood sideboard, the family's traditional red tea set awaited us. Embossed with the "double happiness" symbol, I knew that Māmā would have prepared the teapot with black tea sweetened with dried longans, lotus seeds and red dates.

I had already schooled Matthew on the protocol, and he had been a willing student, so he knew that this ceremony was a way for us to express our respect, gratitude and appreciation for our parents' love and support throughout our childhood years.

First of all, we knelt in front of his parents, Robert and Martha. They smiled as Ling handed us the teacups so that we could serve tea to my in-laws.

"Please drink tea," we said together, and Robert and Martha solemnly took the cups and proceeded to sip from them. Robert then handed us a red envelope containing money as a blessing of our union.

Then we served Māmā and Bàba their tea, offering the same formality and reverence. Again, we received a red envelope as an official blessing of our union.

Before long, we had served Nǎinai and all of our uncles and aunts on both sides. Each time we received our red envelope, Ju took them from us to put them somewhere safe until after the wedding.

"My knees are aching," Matthew whispered out of the corner of his mouth.

"Shhhhh," I giggled. "You're doing brilliantly!"

Once the tea ceremony was concluded, I turned to Matthew and beamed up at him. "See you at the church!"

With that, Filipa, Ju and Ling ushered me out of the room and up the stairs, ready to help me into my second outfit of the day: my very white, very American, wedding dress.

Made from beautiful organza, it had a corseted bodice with a sweetheart neckline, and intricate flowers had been embroidered all over with white thread, in the center of which were lustrous, tiny white pearls. Cinched in at the waist by the corset, the A-line skirt flared out beautifully at the bottom, and I felt like a queen. As soon as I had seen this dress, I had fallen in love with it, and even Māmā had made little fuss about the neckline once she had seen me in it.

There was a knock on my bedroom door just as Ling was tying the ribbons of the corset. Bàba had come to collect me to lead me to the car.

"Gūniáng ... you are ready?" he asked as he came into the room. "Ling, Ju, Filipa ... please leave us."

Ling gave my hand a squeeze, and then she left with the others as Bàba came to stand in front of me. He gazed at me in my gown and nodded his head in approval.

"I know that your mother and I weren't happy at first about your intention to marry Matthew," he said, "but we can see that the boy is good for you, even if he's not Chinese!" He put his hand up to stop me from interrupting. "I know … I know. You needed to marry for *love*, and we understand that now. We've grown to become quite attached to him too, you know?

"You've always been a good girl, Mei, and we want you to know that we are proud of you, our daughter. Now go … be happy!"

I flung my arms around my father and felt him freeze at the unexpected act of affection, but then he raised his arms and gave me an awkward squeeze in return. "Come now," he said, "less of that or we'll crumple your dress, and what would your mother say about that?" Then, offering me his arm, he led me downstairs and out onto the street, where the most gorgeous white car was waiting to take me to church.

"Wait a minute, please," I said as the chauffeur opened the door for me. "I forgot something!"

Ignoring my family's confused mutterings, I lifted my skirts and ran around the side of the house to the back yard. Stopping in front of Ai's bush, I stooped and plucked a rose.

"I need a part of you with me today, Ai," I said as I tucked the bloom into the center of my bouquet. The violet flower popped against the white roses nestled in the dark green foliage, and now I knew that I was ready.

爱

Waiting for me outside the church was Wing—who was one of the ushers—Ling, Ju and Filipa.

"You look beautiful, jiějiě," Wing said as he kissed me on the cheek. "You ready?" As I gave him a grateful smile, I nodded my head. With a fair amount of gusto, he opened the church doors wide, revealing the narrow aisle that led to the altar where Matthew would be waiting. "Good luck!"

Upon Wing's signal, the organist stopped what he had been playing and instead began blasting out Mendelssohn's "Wedding March." Every head in the congregation turned to look at me, and I felt myself hesitate.

"Matthew's just at the other end of the aisle, jiějiě," Ling whispered. "Eyes front, one step in front of the other, and go and marry your man. We're right here behind you!"

So, I took my first few steps down the

aisle, holding on for dear life to Bàba's arm, all the while keeping my eyes fixed on the altar. I couldn't see Matthew yet, but I could see the rector, who was smiling as I approached.

And then Matthew stepped forwards to meet me, and everything else faded away. As our eyes connected, my anxiety dissipated, and I longed to be next to him. I heard Filipa chuckle behind me as my footsteps quickened in my urgency to reach him, and I felt my father tug at my hand to slow my pace once more.

I couldn't take my eyes off him. He looked so beautiful in his white tuxedo, and then I gasped as I noted the violet rose in his lapel. He smiled and gave me a wink.

"Who gives this woman to be married here today?" the rector asked.

"I do," Bàba said as he offered my hand to Matthew. With a kiss to my cheek and a slap to Matthew's shoulder, Bàba then went to join Māmā in the front pew.

"I love you, Rose. So much," Matthew whispered as he gazed deep into my eyes, and I could feel his hand trembling as it held mine. I gave it a squeeze.

I turned to the rector and whispered a request before facing my groom once more and holding both of his hands in mine. I didn't hear most of the introduction to the wedding ceremony—I was too lost in Matthew—but a little cough from the rector soon let me know that it was time for our vows.

"Do you, Matthew James, take Mei-Rose Shu to be your lawfully wedded wife?" the rector said as I smiled at Matthew's raised eyebrow upon hearing my name. "Do you promise to love her, honor her, cherish and protect her for as long as you both shall live?"

"I do," said Matthew, grinning. "Mei-Rose?" he mouthed to me.

"And do you, Mei-Rose Shu, take Matthew James to be your lawfully wedded husband? Do you promise to love him, honor him, cherish and protect him for as long as you both shall live?"

"I do!" I said.

"Then, by the power invested in me, I proclaim you to be husband and wife! You may seal your union with a kiss."

Matthew stepped forward and lifted my veil before cupping my face in his two hands. I felt the raspberry blush creep up my neck at the thought of such an intimate act as a kiss being performed in front of my family and friends, but Matthew understood. Leaning towards me, he placed a chaste kiss upon my lips and then turned to face the congregation. Lifting up our joined hands, he beamed at all of our loved ones.

The organ began belting out "All You Need is Love," and the congregation stood and began applauding as we made our way out of the church. It felt as though I were walking on clouds as I held the hand of the man whom I adored.

爱

The wedding banquet was held at the Four Seasons Hotel, and it was set to be a lavish affair. Intent on fusing Chinese culture with American, Matthew and I had worked tirelessly to produce a menu and décor to show off both. Set in the ballroom of the hotel, we were certainly blessed with a beautifully appointed canvas with which to work.

The circular tables for the guests had been draped with red tablecloths, and they had white origami phoenix place cards for people's names. Upon each table was a tall glass vase containing beautiful and fragrant white roses, which were set against deep green lemon leaf and draping ivy vines. Three low, white pillar candles on each table provided the ambient lighting, which partnered beautifully with the sconces on the walls.

The long wedding party table was positioned by the far wall and was decorated in much the same way. Behind it, and hanging from gold ribbon, was the double happiness symbol, which had been created using 100 red roses. It took my breath away as we sat to begin our banquet.

Matthew had been astounded when I had told him that our wedding feast needed eight courses. But, as a man who loved his food, he really had no objection. He was fast becoming used to the symbolism involved in many of the Chinese traditions.

When designing our menu, I had chosen auspicious foods that represented abundance, peace, unity and my purity in the Chinese culture. Yet, we had made sure that lots of these foods had an American twist to them too.

We began the wedding feast with the soup course that Matthew and I had organized—a Cantonese slow-cooked soup. But, I was more than surprised when Nǎinai came hobbling over to us with a soup flask in one hand and two empty bowls in the other.

"Eat this, not that!" she said to us in Cantonese as she handed each of us an empty bowl.

"Nǎinai? What are you doing?" I asked.

"This soup is for you," she said grinning at me with a glint in her eye. "Bone broth!"

"No ..." I moaned as realization dawned and my face flushed. "Nǎinai!"

"What is it?" Matthew asked, clearly amused by how uncomfortable I was. I groaned as Nǎinai looked between the two of us in anticipation.

"Bone broth," I said to him. "It's ... *errrrm* ... it's, well ... we use it in Chinese culture for ... *errrrm* ..."

Matthew started to laugh. "For what?"

"Fertility," I mumbled as Matthew's eyes widened.

"Pardon me?"

My face was on fire. "We use it in Chinese culture to help with fertility."

"Oh!" he said, laughing as he lifted his spoon. "Right then. Well ... eat up!"

爱

Following the first four courses of soup, fish, duck and suckling pig, it was time to cut the cake. Auntie Bunty had insisted on making it for us as her wedding gift, and it was a work of art.

Four tiers high, the bottom and second tier

The Origami Balloon

were wrapped with red fondant, and the third and top tiers were layered with white icing. The white tiers she had left plain, save for small subtle sugar pearls that encircled each, but the red tiers were an oriental masterpiece of golden double happiness symbols, phoenixes and dragons.

Upon the top tier, Auntie Bunty had crafted sugar ornament versions of me and Matthew wearing our church outfits. It was almost too phenomenal to cut. Almost. Each tier was also a different flavor of cake: fruit, red velvet, chocolate and vanilla sponge.

After we had cut the cake and been blinded by all of the camera flashes, Ling came to find me.

"Outfit change!" she said with relish.

"*Aiiii-ya*! Again?" I moaned. I had never changed so much in my life before, and I was finding it tiresome.

"Of course! It's time for your qipao!"

So, leaving the guests to chat between courses, I went upstairs to the bridal suite where Ju and Filipa were waiting to help me into my traditional Chinese wedding dress. Even though I was feeling grumpy because of yet another change of clothes, I had to admit that my trumpet-style qipao was gorgeous. With a high collar and cap sleeves, it was made from a beautiful red lace which also trailed out as a train behind me.

The effect was finished off by several golden bangles on both wrists, and Ling secured a 24-carat golden pig, which hung from a beautifully intricate chain, around my neck.

"Beautiful!" Ju said as she gave me a hug.

Back at the banquet, Matthew shook his head in disbelief as I walked towards him. "Each time you change, you look more and more beautiful," he said as he pulled me into an embrace and nuzzled my neck. "Or ... maybe it's Năinai's soup taking effect already!"

"Stop!" I laughed as I felt the heat return to my cheeks.

Once we reached the final course of sweet lotus seed dessert, a slideshow of mine and Matthew's childhood photographs began to play on the projector screen, much to our embarrassment but to the guests' delight.

And then it was time for us to leave. The guests would dance on into the night if they so wished, but it was time for my husband to take me home.

As Matthew drove my yellow Bug off down the street, the guests stood outside to cheer us off. They laughed at the tin cans that Filipa and Ling had attached to the bumper and the "Just Married!" sprayed onto the back window in shaving foam by Wing. I couldn't have been happier.

Pulling up outside our new home, which was three streets away from where I had grown up, Matthew turned to face me in the car.

"Welcome home, Mrs. Moore! Are you happy?"

"I don't think I could be any happier, Mr. Moore," I said, and I leaned across and kissed my husband the way I had been waiting to kiss him all day. "I love you so much." Grinning at me, he then jumped out of his side of the car and rushed around to open my door.

Helping me out of the Beetle, Matthew then scooped me up into his arms as it began to rain, and he jogged with me up the path to the front door.

"Ah ... the keys!" he said as raindrops trickled down his face. "They're in my pocket! Can you reach them?"

Laughing, I fumbled in his pocket to retrieve the keys. Once I had managed to open the door, despite my awkward position, Matthew carried me with flair across the threshold, only to trip on the doormat, which sent us both careering to the floor in a soggy, tangled heap and a fit of giggles.

"*Mmmm* ... hello," Matthew then murmured into my damp hair, changing the mood in an instant.

"Hi," I breathed back, gazing into his eyes as he leaned over me to push the door shut with his hand, shutting out the world beyond.

And as the rain lashed against the windows and the sunset cast its orangey-golden hues through gaps in the gray clouds across the city's rooftops, I finally came to realize how beautiful it was to be loved so deeply, so absolutely, by someone who had gifted me their heart for an eternity.

自爱

Epilogue

The most amazing sound in the world is the sound of a child laughing, especially when that child is your own. As I leaned against the doorframe, looking out over my back yard, I couldn't help but laugh too as I watched my six-year-old daughter throw a stick for Xing, our dog.

Xing had claimed my little family as her own, much as Ai had done many, many years before. The winter after Melanie had turned four, we had discovered the dog curled up on our back doorstep, and she had been almost frozen. Matthew had immediately brought her into the kitchen to warm her by the range, and young Melanie wouldn't leave her alone. After that, the dog was given a permanent bed by the cooker and an unwavering place in our hearts.

We had named her Xing because she had a white star-like mark in the fur on her head despite the rest of her being jet black. And as the bond between Xing and Melanie had deepened

The Origami Balloon

over the last two years, it was clear that Xing was going to be the guiding star to Melanie as Ai had been to me.

Xing emerged from the shrubbery and bounded back to my daughter, knocking her over in her unabashed enthusiasm to have the stick thrown again.

"You okay, sweetheart?" I called out, although my concern wasn't necessary as I could hear Melanie giggling as Xing tried to lick her face.

"I'm fine, Māmā," she said.

"Well, come on," I said, "It's time to get ready. Daddy will be home soon, and it's nearly time for the baby reveal party."

I rubbed my hand over my swollen abdomen and felt little flutterings as the baby moved to a more comfortable position. Today we would find out whether we were having a boy or another girl. I didn't mind either way, so long as the baby was healthy.

"Did I hear my name?" Matthew said as he came to stand behind me, kissing my cheek and putting his arms around me to rub my stomach.

"Daddy! You're home!" Melanie squealed as she ran to greet him, and Xing barked happily as she tangled herself up in Melanie's legs.

"Hello, ragamuffin!" Matthew laughed as he threw Melanie up into the air and then caught her safely in his arms. "You, my girl, need a bath!" he said as he looked at the smudges of dirt covering her face and the bits of leaves in her hair. "The family will be here soon, and look at you!" He bent down to pat the dog and then threw Melanie over his shoulder as he headed to the stairs. "You," he turned to me, "take a rest and have a cup of tea. I've got this."

But instead, I went into the dining room to check that the table was prepared. There, center-stage, was the beautiful white cake that Auntie Bunty had made for us—she was the only one who knew the gender of the baby growing inside me.

Auntie Bunty had retired from the bakery five years ago, and she had bequeathed it to me. Although she remained a silent partner in the business, she had been adamant that the premises became mine to launch my own bakery of Chinese-American fusion delicacies. I regularly blessed my lucky stars for that day, all those years ago, when I had happened upon *Bunty's Cookies and Cakes* tucked down that little side street. Auntie Bunty had become like another grandmother to me, and I could never thank her enough for everything that she had done for me.

"You deserve it all," she would say to me when I tried to share my gratitude. "You're an absolute treasure, Mei-Rose, and you've worked hard for this. No thanks are needed!" But still, I tried.

Anyway, we had asked Melanie to assign a color to each potential gender of her new sibling. Auntie Bunty had told me that she'd then used the correct color for the butter cream inside the cake based on the scan photographs we had given her in the sealed envelope: purple for a girl and green for a boy. As I looked at the cake now, nothing about it gave the gender away, and my fingers itched to take the knife and slice a little bit off to see ... but no. I had waited this long, after all.

I went back into the kitchen to check on the items cooking in the oven. Glancing at the clock, I realized that Ling and her husband, Donghai, would be arriving soon, as my little sister had promised to help me finish setting up. Recently married, Ling was still experiencing the "honeymoon period" and positively glowed in her happiness.

Māmā and Bàba would be bringing Nǎinai, who was well into her 90s but who stayed spritely for the sake of her great grandchildren—her pride and joy. Robert and Martha would be there with Matthew's sister and her family, and Wing had traveled over from New York the day before with Baozhai—his lovely wife, who was also into dinosaurs—and their two-year-old son, Tao.

Wing had managed to secure his dream job. He now worked at the Paleontological Research Institution researching dinosaurs and sharing his vast wisdom with his many interns. This was where he had met Baozhai. It was a far cry from our childhood days when Māmā used to take us to visit the National History Museum as children, but it had been there that his love for the prehistoric behemoths had ignited. My brother was so happy, and this made me so thankful.

Ju, Huan, their two young sons and their baby daughter were coming with Auntie Lian and Uncle Bao, who had recently needed emergency heart bypass surgery, giving us all quite the scare. Fortunately, he was recovering well and getting right under Auntie Lian's feet at home.

"I need him back at work," she would laugh. "He makes the place untidy!"

I was so excited to see them all, yet as I stirred the rice, my mind wandered to one of the people who I would miss most today: Yéyé. I hoped that my grandfather would be proud of the person I had become as he looked down on me from where he was.

And Filipa would be missing from this celebration too. My friend had married a Spaniard the year after my own wedding, and she and Luis had moved to Cádiz a few months ago to start a new life there. We had promised to visit each other regularly, or as often as we could, but it was strange to be so far apart from her after all of the years we'd had together.

Quickly, I gave myself a shake; today was meant to be full of happy thoughts …

Xing had picked up on my somberness, and as I sat down in one of the kitchen chairs to take the weight off my feet, she came over and laid her head in my lap. She gazed up at me with her beautiful brown eyes as I scratched behind her ears.

"You remind me so much of him, you know?" I said to her.

Xing lifted her head and tilted it to one side as though she wanted to show that she was listening.

"I knew another dog once … one with a heart of gold," I said as I smiled sadly. "He helped me to learn who I wanted to be. I miss him *so* much!"

Xing stood up on her back legs with her front paws resting on my knees, head still cocked, and she looked deep into my eyes. Then she leaned forwards and licked me with her slobbery tongue from my chin to my forehead, and I burst out laughing.

"Yep! He used to do that too," I chuckled, wiping my face with my sleeve as Xing gave a little bark and then started to chase her tail, clearly overjoyed that she had managed to cheer me up.

"Jiějiě? Are you here?" called Ling from the hallway before she came bustling into the kitchen with the bags of groceries that I had forgotten to get. "Right," she said as she kissed me on the cheek, "Where shall I start?"

爱

It felt like we were cutting our wedding cake all over again—it really was that exciting! Everyone's eyes were on us as we held the knife together, poised to cut the sweet delight that would reveal if our baby was a boy or a girl. With his other arm, Matthew gave my shoulder a squeeze.

"Ready?" he said.

"Oh *come on*, Daddy, Māmā!" called out Melanie. "I want to know now! I want it to be a sister!"

"Ready," I said to Matthew, and we cut into the cake.

As we removed the slice, the purple butter cream was clear to see, but just in case that hadn't been enough of a clue, Auntie Bunty had filled the center of the cake with purple sweets too, which now came pouring out like a sugary waterfall.

"It's a sister! It's a sister!" chanted Melanie as she came over and hugged my legs, and everyone began to cheer and clap.

"Měilì de! Another little great granddaughter," Năinai murmured to my mother as she smiled through her tears. "How lovely!" Māmā patted her hand gently.

"You happy it's a girl?" I said to Matthew as everyone else began chatting amongst themselves again. "You aren't sad it's not a boy?"

"I'm thrilled!" he promised me. "Another little you, and another little Melanie ... how can I *not* be delighted with that?" He pulled me into a hug and kissed me soundly on the lips. "Besides, who says we're stopping at two?" he said as he winked at me.

"*Eww* ... Daddy and Māmā are *kissing*!"

Melanie said to her cousin, and Matthew lunged for her as she squealed in delight.

"And anyway," he said as he tickled a squirming but giggling Melanie on his hip, "maybe I can speak to Năinai about tweaking that bone broth for us? You know … maybe she can add a special 'make a boy' herb or two to it?"

Then he laughed out loud as I looked at him in horror before aiming a steamed bun at his head, much to the disapproval of my mother.

"Broth?" said Năinai. "Did someone mention broth?"

"No, Năinai," I said, glowering at Matthew, who just blew me a kiss, "it's okay!"

"*Aiiii-ya!*" she said as she shuffled off. "I wish the youngsters would stop mumbling!"

So there I was, surrounded by my family, surrounded by love. I placed my hands on my stomach and felt the baby move again. We were bringing her into a world that made sense to me once again.

I hoped beyond hope that she and Melanie would always see the beauty in the people around them, and that they would always appreciate the magical diversity of their roots. It would forever be mine and Matthew's unique gift to our precious children. Our legacy of unconditional love, just for them.

The Origami Balloon

自爱

Acknowledgements

Firstly, I would like to thank my husband, Don. He is truly my pillar of strength and my best friend. He encouraged me to write my book, and this was a remarkable breakthrough for both of us. Thank you, Don, for believing in me.

I would like to thank my parents and my family, those living in the US and abroad. Thank you for your love, concern and care for me. You make me smile.

I would also like to thank Pashmina P. and the OAO (Online Author's Office) team for their expertise and support. When I met Pashmina, I knew that we had chemistry, and we connected through the similar ideals we had growing up as third culture kids. I always look forward to seeing Pashmina on our Zoom calls, and her team at the OAO is an outstanding group of individuals who always show care and compassion and who are spot on with their advice.

I am eternally grateful for Charlotte L. Taylor as my editorial and literary advisor. Without her expertise, I wouldn't have known where to start. She held my hand every step of the way, and her professionalism is immaculate. Thank you, Charlie, for your wisdom and knowledge.

I would like to thank the mentors who've guided me thus far. You gave me the strength to find my passion. The road is not easy sometimes, but when you find that sweet spot in your heart that leads the way, the rest of the journey can only be described as magical.

Helena M. Craggs. Thank you for taking the time to beta read my book and for falling in love with Mei and her journey. I appreciate you.

Lastly, thank you to my readers for picking up my book. I hope that you find some messages within the pages that resonate with you and help you on your own personal journey.

About the Author

Cheryl Moy lives with her husband in the heart of Chicago, Illinois, and she runs a successful business in insurance. However, she has always had a fascination with the structure of different societies, and she graduated her college years from the University of Northern Illinois with a BA degree in Sociology.

Cheryl has always had the propensity to help others—this is part of her very core—and her dream is to become a coach, helping people to embrace who they are. Her vision sees her reaching those who face daily battles with their inner voice telling them that they are not good enough. Cheryl wants everyone to understand that their well-being is as important as their physical health, so this too needs to be nurtured.

"Learn to love yourself first, and then you will have the gift of joy to spread to others."
—*Cheryl Moy.*

The Origami Balloon: Becoming Mei-Rose is Cheryl's debut novel, and its completion sees another one of her life goals accomplished.